TRUE BLUE DETECTIVE SERIES BOOK FOUR

STREET JUSTICE

Street Justice

This book is a work of fiction. Names, characters, businesses, organizations, places, events, and incidents are the product of the author's imagination.

Published by Vito Zuppardo.

TRUE BLUE DETECTIVE SERIES BOOK FOUR

STREET JUSTICE

VITO ZUPPARDO

WHAT READERS ARE SAYING

TRUE BLUE DETECTIVE SERIES

Five Stars: Super Book
I enjoyed this book. I am not usually into this mystery book, but the blurb on this one caught my attention. It is well worth the time to read. It is well written and has lots of action and adventure.

Five Stars: Intriguing, keeps you on the edge of your seat
Very good read. This keeps you nearly at your seat. Plus it describes various parts of the city of New Orleans, which is wonderful if you've never been.

Five Stars: A Wonderful Book!
This was a great book. I loved the plot and the characters. I read this book in one sitting. I enjoyed the plot. It was full of excitement and intrigue.

ALSO BY
VITO ZUPPARDO

TRUE BLUE DETECTIVE SERIES

True Blue Detective
Crescent City Detective
Vieux Carré Detective
Street Justice

VOODOO LUCY SERIES

Tupelo Gypsy
Revenge

LADY LUCK SERIES

Alluring Lady Luck (2015)
Tales of Lady Luck (2016)

At the end of this book,
read two chapters of *Revenge*, book two in the Voodoo Lucy series, and get *Tupelo Gypsy*, book one in the Voodoo Lucy series, FREE.

Go to
www.vitozuppardobooks.com

CHAPTER 1

GOOD DETECTIVES KEEP A keen eye on their surroundings. Mario DeLuca is that detective.

Mario's morning run took him deep into the French Quarter. A coffee break at the three-mile mark, he'd sit his sweaty body on the patio of the Roasted Bean Café, a courtesy to the early morning work crowd neatly dressed, getting their caffeine to go.

His break, never over fifteen minutes, was just long enough for his muscles and body to cool down. Even with the occasional glance from an attractive woman two tables down, it was still time to go. She'd glance and look away as a high school teenager would, but she wasn't. She checked all the boxes for Mario. Tall, lean body, fair complexion, blue eyes, and reddish hair. Her top, shorts, and shoes identified her as a runner. By his calculations, it would be an easy score for a phone number. Striking up a conversation about her jogging routine would have opened the door for dialog and the possibility of a lunch date, if he only had the time.

She glanced again, this time with a smile, then a

flirtatious grin. Mario had no one in his life. He and Olivia were too much into their jobs to be anything other than buddies to have drinks with, although they had been intimate discreetly—both being cops.

Taking out four, one-dollar bills, rolled tightly in his sock, and placing them on the table, he gave the signal of a hand wave to the waitress.

She acknowledged with a smile. "Thank you, Mario."

He'd continued to the door, questioning himself, at forty-two-years old, if he needed to make use of every opportunity to meet a woman, especially a knockout like her. How else would he ever settle down with a wife, have kids, a house, and maybe a dog?

Before he could get to the iron gate exiting to the street, a tap on his shoulder got his attention. Mario, speechless when he turned around, gazed into the blue eyes of the female jogger.

"Hi, I'm Adrianna." A beautiful smile and shiny white teeth greeted him.

Mario introduced himself and shook her hand. "Can I help you?"

"Possibly." Tossing a small workout bag on a table, she took a seat. "I see you're a runner."

Mario followed like a puppy dog, sat across from her, and snickered. She'd used the same line he would have if he'd taken a shot at striking up a conversation.

"What kind of work do you do?"

Mario dodged being a homicide cop and said, "I'm an investment banker."

"What about you?"

"Before we go into me," she said and tossed her head, letting her hair flop from side to side. Mario's eyes and mind fixated on the words across her shirt, "Run Hard."

She directed him to look into her eyes. "Let's talk about you. You're a cop in charge of the Eighth District, Homicide Division. Your right-hand man is Truman, and you're the love interest of Olivia."

Mario's thoughts flipped in his mind, rapidly. Was she a witness in a case, the wife of a murdered husband, or a first-rate starker? "Have we met?"

"No." She unzipped the tote bag and rummaged. "Carefully, I want you to look inside."

Mario bent over the table and peeked in the bag. Her hand was wrapped around a handgun with a silencer suppressor. It was pointed at him. He abruptly sat down. His mind went into cop mode, eyes canvassing a way out. With no one getting hurt.

"While you were engrossed, watching my hair flop around, gawking at my chest, I could have put two bullets in your head."

"What do you want?"

"I'm a messenger. Helena Acosta wants the cartel's money, all twelve million dollars."

"Or what? You'll kill me?" His training, keep her talking, was the only defense.

"You have forty-eight hours." The bag tossed over her shoulder, she left a business card. "I got the drop on you once. Next time it won't be pleasant."

CHAPTER 2

THE RUN BACK WAS usually a slow jog, but this morning Mario was in full sprint to his condo. Straight across Canal Street, running around an oncoming streetcar to keep his pace. His mind raced faster than his feet were moving.

Transferring the Savino family money to an offshore account was meant to cripple Lorenzo Savino's drug empire. Mario and Howard Blitz, an undercover cop, intended to turn the twelve million over to the FBI. The delay was a plausible reason it was in their possession.

Mario arrived at his building short-winded. He stood at the entrance to catch his breath, when a man walked down the steps, turned the corner, and was quickly out of sight.

Such a well-dressed man, Mario noticed first, suit and tie, thin mustache, slick hair, and he had a skip in his step. He'd never seen him in the building before, but with seventy-five apartments over three floors, he didn't know everyone, he convinced himself. Could be a boyfriend of one of the single women living on the top floor, rushing to get home to his wife. He didn't put it past those women to romance a married man.

Jimmy Wells, the doorman who preferred to be called

Junior, wasn't in the lobby, odd for that time of the morning. Chatty Junior, Mario nicknamed him after he was hired. He talked entirely too much. Just good morning or afternoon was all Mario wanted to hear out of a doorman.

The elevator door opened. Mario stepped in, when a thought hit him. He'd not seen Junior on his way out for his run.

Mario caught the doors before they closed, exited the elevator, and walked the lobby. He gave out a shout for Junior a few times. Checked the men's restroom and knocked on the ladies restroom before checking inside it too. From the storage room, a muffled sound and a kick at the door got Mario's attention.

Carefully, he tried to turn the door handle. It was locked, so he forced it open to find Junior sitting on a mop bucket, gagged, and hands tied behind his back.

A few minutes later, Junior sat on a couch in the lobby gathering his thoughts, while Mario fetched him coffee from the concierge lounge. A few sips were allowed before Mario bombarded him with questions, his cop mode was in full bloom.

"Start from the beginning, Junior."

His morning started the same every day. Placing newspapers in the stand next to the elevator. The bakery delivered doughnuts and pastries, and he set them up in the concierge lounge. Then he made fresh coffee. When he exited the lounge, he was taken from behind by what felt like a gun to his back. Then gagged, tied up, and locked in the storage room. He couldn't tell if it was one or more people involved and never saw a face nor did anyone speak.

Mario called it in, and within seconds, three police cars were on the scene. There was nothing more to the report, but there had to be a reason for the attack on Junior. A police lieutenant arrived and took charge. In consideration for a fellow officer and resident of the building, the lieutenant called for cops to go floor by floor and knock on every door, making sure everyone was safe.

Mario headed to his apartment. A quick shower was needed. The lieutenant kept Mario informed by radio. Everyone was accounted for on the first floor. Apartments where no one was home, Junior let the cops in with his master key. Under extreme circumstances, it was allowable for him to open an apartment for the police. This was one such time.

Mario joined the police on his floor to continue the search, and still there were no problems. It became puzzling to Mario why Junior was accosted. Now, the detective focused on Junior. He had a list of questions, maybe he had gambling debts or drug problems. Mario flashed back to the security check on Jimmy Wells; he ran it himself. It came up clean, unless Junior was using an alias.

An officer informed Mario that every room was accounted for except apartment 221; there was no answer. Mario knew Dale, he'd lived in the building for two years with his girlfriend. He wasn't sure of Dale's last name but knew he was the manager of a fancy Italian restaurant in the French Quarter.

Mario gave a knock at the door and shouted for Dale; there was no response. He called for Junior with the master key. Mario gave it another shot, banging and shouting Dale's name, then Junior opened the door.

Two officers roamed the apartment. Mario stood in the living room, admiring either Dale or his girlfriend's painting of famous buildings in the French Quarter. "Someone is a good artist."

"Detective," an officer shouted from the bedroom, "in here!"

Mario heard the officer make a radio call for paramedics. "Female alive. Male dead."

Things moved quickly, and the room was soon flooded with police. There were police in the street to flag down the paramedics and a cop at the elevator holding the door open on the ground floor.

Mario, on his knees, pulled the woman's hair back from her face. She was pressing on a gunshot wound to her stomach. She whispered, but Mario couldn't make out what she said.

"You're going to be okay."

"Mario?"

"I'm here." He stroked her hand to keep her calm.

Mario heard the elevator bell when the doors opened on the floor. The clanging sound of a gurney and people rushing toward them.

The woman pulled Mario by the shirt. "I told the guy Dale wasn't Mario, but he shot him anyway."

CHAPTER 3

ROBERTO FERRARI TIPPED HIS hat to people when he entered his place of business. Roberto was popular among women as the fellow with a boyish smile and devilish eyes. Always dressed impressively in a brimmed, straw fedora in the summer, down to his shiny wingtip shoes. Years had passed and Roberto, a handsome man of sixty, still got attention from the ladies. The women who were ten years younger, he'd call "girls"—and they loved it. Some said it was his good looks, others said it was his power since he took over as head of the family business.

The Atlantic City Boardwalk was full of tourists this time of year, and they flocked to Ferrari's Italian Restaurant. Established by his Sicilian grandparents sixty-five years ago, it was now owned by the third generation. Roberto used the place for his office. A round table that seated ten acted as a desk in the rear of the restaurant where most business decisions were made. Extortion, drug deals, who lived, who died, and plans for the future. Roberto Ferrari, the head of a New Jersey crime family, had many responsibilities and someone had to answer for the death of one of his top earners, Lorenzo Savino.

A black Lincoln Town Car waited outside the baggage claim area of the Philadelphia airport. The driver spotted his passenger, Michael Ferrari, a known member of Roberto's crew.

Michael sat in the front seat, and before saying a word, he pulled the vanity mirror down, checked his hair, and smoothed his mustache.

"Good flight?"

"Yes, in and out quickly." Michael eyes, still glued to the mirror, were more engrossed in his hair than conversation.

Nothing more was said during the hour drive to Atlantic City. Michael was dropped off as close to the Boardwalk as possible and walked the short distance to the restaurant. He spotted Roberto at his table with his right-hand man, Bobby G. Only a crew member like Michael would notice the three bodyguards dressed as waiters who hung around the rear of the room. They had one job, and that was keeping Roberto safe.

"Boss?" They hugged it out, and Michael took a seat.

"You're done?" Bobby G. always got to the point, never small talk.

"Yep." Michael showed a proud grin. "A girl got in the way. But I handled her."

"No witnesses?" Bobby G. watched to see if he flinched at the question. He didn't.

Roberto made a hand gesture, and a waiter poured coffee and placed a platter of Italian cookies on the table. "Have some."

"Grandma's fig cookies." Michael put two on a plate. "She always made the best."

Roberto's smile showed his white capped teeth. "Yes, she did. So everything went as planned?"

"Sure, boss." Michael tugged at his belt and moved it up an inch or two.

"Then, why is Mario DeLuca still alive?" A hand slammed the table. His voice elevated and a vein puffed on his forehead just below where the rim of his hat sat.

"What are you talking about?" Michael watched from the corner of his eye, expecting them to go into a roaring laugh, as they often did with their sick jokes. "No way he's alive. I took the doorman by surprise, climbed the steps, and knocked on apartment 221. A woman answered; I expected a love interest for that time of the morning. With my gun to her back, we walked to the bedroom, and I put three in Mario's chest and two in the girl." He rocked on the back legs of his chair. "Come on, guys, a little praise for a job well done."

"Did you leave the evidence?"

"Yes, in the trash can, the bedroom, and on the dining room table."

"One problem." Roberto's face was beet red, the vein doubled in size. "Mario DeLuca lives in apartment 212. You dyslexic bastard."

Michael pulled a piece of paper from his pocket. He looked twice, but it was clear he'd hit the wrong apartment. "I'll go back. I can make this right."

Roberto shook his head in a downward position and reached for another cookie. Taking a bite, slowly chewing, like he was savoring the taste. His eyes peered into space; one could almost see the devil dancing in his eyes.

Michael had seen this look before, and it didn't end well. He didn't want to be that person. "Boss, I'll handle this. I promise!"

Roberto chewing, at times spitting crumbs, went into a vocal fury. Two bodyguards closed the glass doors. His voice had carried into the restaurant and heads turned.

The plan had been to kill Mario in his apartment. Make it look like a hit, a bookmaker or a drug deal gone bad.

Michael continued to plead his case and went into detail about how he could fix the problem. His mouth rattled out crap it couldn't back up, but he'd say anything to convince the boss he was worthy of making good on his promise.

"This was carefully planned." Roberto slowly crept around the table, but his eyes fixed on Michael. "In the apartment, Mario is a resident of the community. Everyone would question his death, but the evidence would indicate he was a dirty cop. Kill him on the street, he's a brother in blue, and every police officer in New Orleans will come down on us."

Michael didn't make eye contact. His only thought was how to get out of the room alive. His gun was someplace at the bottom of the Mississippi River. The sole purpose of taking a ferry ride across the river from New Orleans to Algiers. Wouldn't matter anyway; he couldn't shoot his way out of this problem.

Roberto sat and calmed himself, taking a sip of coffee, which was once hot. "Okay, call that gal Lorenzo was so high on." Pointing a finger at Bobby G.

"Julie Wong?" Bobby G's eyebrow raised. "She's expensive. Fifty thousand, last I checked."

"Doesn't matter. I'm not paying." Roberto turned to Michael with a look of evil. It would scare anyone. "You'll pay." His arms wrapped around Michael's neck.

"Not a problem, boss." He knew better than to fight the headlock.

Roberto tightened his arms. "If you weren't my nephew—you'd be dead."

Michael's mother had died of natural causes at an early age, so he was told. His father died a year ago, and the family loyalty was passed to Roberto, the only living sibling of his generation. He controlled everything, including who lived and died.

With pressure on his neck, Michael tried to speak. A squeaky voice pleaded for another chance at Mario. He'd screwed up and had to make good—begging was his only option.

Roberto released him, forcefully slammed his face into the table, and broke the platter of cookies over his head. Blood spilled on the white tablecloth. "Clean up this mess." Then he stormed out the room.

CHAPTER 4

AN INTERVIEW WITH NEIGHBORS shone light on an ex-boyfriend who he was heard deep into a shouting match with the woman found dead in the apartment. Mario wasn't aware of any ruckus. She was identified as Dawn Taylor, and a picture from her wallet showed her and a man at the beach. Two neighbors confirmed the man in the photo was involved in the disturbance.

One person came forward saying Dawn had broken up with the guy two months earlier. She wasn't 100 percent sure of the reason but overheard conversations of him losing a job twice within six months.

The double homicide hit the front page of the newspaper the next morning. Little information was given by a police spokesperson for the ongoing investigation, other than a person of interest was the dead woman's ex-boyfriend. The statement issued indicated it might have been a domestic dispute. No mention of a police officer living in the building.

Mario wanted no part and handed it off to Truman, his former partner, and now number-one detective under his command at the Eighth District.

Two hours later, Truman met at the station with Mario and three, top-ranked detectives. Mario sat at the head of the table and reviewed open cases. He called on Truman first for an update on the apartment murder.

The police had found several daily racing forms and hundreds of dollars of lost betting tickets from the New Orleans Fair Grounds Race Course . On the kitchen table, a newspaper was opened to the sports page with horses circled for the day's races.

Mario looked over the pictures of the evidence taken. "So, he was a gambler?"

"Worse." Truman tossed a photo. "Enough cocaine was found in the apartment to charge with distribution."

Mario suggested they dump the man's cell phone and the girlfriend's too. Check for recent calls and calls to or from the same numbers. One of the senior detectives added they might want to match up all the names connected to the numbers to run through the DEA. If they got a hit, it would allow the case to be reclassified as a drug deal and not a city homicide.

Mario shook his head. "Dale was a clean-cut, working guy. Hard to believe he had a gambling problem and pushed drugs."

Truman read aloud again all the things found in the apartment. The racing tickets spread in three parts of the house, the sports page opened to the horses in the day's race, and the coke found in the top drawer of a nightstand.

"Something is puzzling." All eyes were on Truman. "Overall, the guy's apartment was immaculate. Except for the items mentioned, a dish wasn't out of place, not even a coffee cup in the sink. The racing tickets were all from yesterday's event." He arranged five tickets on the table. "Look at these tickets. Who bets four horses to win in the same race?"

The new information got everyone's attention. One detective showed where the amounts weren't the norm either. One ticket was for two dollars, another for twenty dollars, and a few for one hundred dollars. His opinion—someone went to the racetrack, scooped up lost tickets from the floor, and planted them in the apartment.

"That's not all. The brick in the drawer had no fingerprints. Was the guy cautious and wore gloves? Then stashed it where it could easily be found?" Truman wanted to check into it further before turning things over to the DEA. It looked like a setup. But why?

CHAPTER 5

MARIO PICKED UP HOWARD at police headquarters and drove to the airport. All Howard knew was that Julie Wong needed to speak to Mario. Her words urgently made him a little uneasy. They discussed Lorenzo's family money or the cartel's money. At this point, they weren't sure who to return the money to or if that was the best move.

Mario had been in touch with Ralph Givens, his con-artist friend turned investment broker. The same business that almost got him twenty years in federal prison. Mario promised he'd never help him again, but this time it was Mario who called on the slimeball for assistance. "I spoke to Ralph. He's been monitoring the Panama bank, and his contacts say there have been no inquiries regarding Lorenzo's money gone missing. All twelve million is safe."

Howard drove and kept glancing at Mario. "We have to make a decision soon. Before one of us is dead, or both. I don't think your jogger friend was bluffing."

Mario gave a nod. He'd been asking his underground snitches, but had no leads on her name or description. A hundred-dollar bounty should get results soon.

The limousine parked at General Aviation and waited for Julie Wong's aircraft to land. The long, sleek body of a Gulfstream jet was seen on approach as it hovered over the lake, as if it was stopped mid-air. Then the thrust of the engine sounded and pushed the plane to a safe landing. It taxied near the limousine. With the engines shut down, a stairway came from within the body of the aircraft and rested on the ground. Julie, dressed perfectly for the New Orleans climate and looking stunning as usual, strolled down the steps like she was walking the red carpet of a Hollywood premiere.

"Gentlemen." She gave them each a peck on the cheek.

Howard opened the rear door of the limousine. She smiled and suggested they move to the airplane. It was more comfortable, and the crew had lunch ready.

"What's so important?" Mario spoke, before hitting the top of the steps.

She turned back to them. "This guy, he's all business—relax."

In the plane, Julie sat at a table, and Mario and Howard took seats on a sofa large enough for four people, so they stretched out. A flight attendant received their drink orders, two coffees. Another attendant pulled solid mahogany wood trays out of the arms of the sofa. The coffees, in beautiful china teacups with saucers, were placed in front of both men.

Julie had water with lemon in a fancy glass and sat at a table facing the men. She thanked the attendants and asked them to give her some privacy.

A fuel truck pulled up next to the airplane. Much like a car at a gas station, the driver unscrewed a cap on top of the wing and pumped fuel.

Julie placed a briefcase on the table, glanced out the window at the truck. "So, Mario? How have you been?"

Mario took a sip of coffee; he never could hide frustration, and his face had a reddish glow. "Why did you drag me out here?"

She peeked out the window a second time. The man topped off the fuel, screwed the cap tightly, and drove off. "Sorry, the smell of the fuel bothers me." She popped the two brass locks on the briefcase, opened it wide enough to slip her hand in, and came out with a gun with a silencer attached. "You see, if I fired the gun while fueling, the vapors might have blown us all up."

Mario and Howard were told to keep their hands away from their pockets. The flight attendant stepped forward and disarmed them both, including the guns and holsters attached to their ankles.

"Julie?" Howard said.

She cut him off. "Hear me out."

Howard shifted his eyes to the side. Mario picked up on it and glanced at the female attendant. If she got closer, he'd grab her and push her toward the gun. It would give Mario a chance at disarming Julie.

"Relax," Julie insisted, but kept the gun pointed.

She asked if they knew the name, Roberto Ferrari. They both said they'd heard the name but knew little about the mafia boss of the East Coast. He was the boss of bosses. Had men in major cities; one city was New Orleans.

Lorenzo Savino had been a self-made man. A member of a crime family with his own crew. Every dollar Lorenzo earned, a piece was kicked up to Mr. Ferrari. "Mario, you killed one of his top earners. Mr. Ferrari is pissed; he wants you dead and hired me for the job. As a witness, I'll have to kill Howard too."

She described Mario's building and his apartment number. He wrinkled his nose at the information she spewed. He'd never talked about his residence with her. Unless Howard did? She kept the gun pointed and stood against the wall. Julie went into details about the man killed at Mario's building a few days earlier. The information she couldn't know, unless she was involved. She explained that the killer botched the plan. Got the apartment numbers mixed up and shot the wrong guy, and to cover it up took out his girlfriend.

Mario's eyes blinked rapidly, glancing at Howard often. His mind raced, reviewing everything he'd ever learned in law enforcement, on the street, and natural instincts about defense when held at gunpoint. But Julie was a professional killer, not some robber trying to steal a wallet.

"Julie, whatever Roberto Ferrari is paying you, we can double." Howard, talking out of character, was pleading for their lives.

With a cocked head, she asked, "Where would cops get that kind of cash?"

"Doesn't matter. It can be done."

"Relax," Julie smiled. Pointing the gun down, she pulled the clip out and released the bullet in the chamber. "Both of you protected me when I most needed your help.

I don't forget my friends. You're lucky the first guy messed up, and Mr. Ferrari hired me to finish the job."

It wasn't easy for the two powerhouse men who fought gangs and criminals of all types to accept they were nearly taken down by a 110-pound woman.

Julie came around the front of the table. "There is a problem, though. Shortly after I was given the job, it was canceled. I'm told Michael talked his way back into his uncle's graces."

"Jesus Christ, Julie!" Howard shouted. "There must have been an easier way to alert us that Ferrari wanted us dead."

"The threat is real. I got to you—anyone can."

All Julie could offer was the name Michael Ferrari as the guy who screwed up the hit at Mario's apartment building. He now had the contract for a second try.

CHAPTER 6

TRUMAN TAGGED ALONG WITH Mario downtown to catch the arraignment for Little Pete Gallo. Other than Angelina "Lina" Savino, who was never charged with a crime, Little Pete was the only remaining Savino family member not in jail.

Mario parked his cruiser across the busy four-lane street just a half block from the courthouse. Mario popped his umbrella as a light rain fell. Truman insisted he'd hoof it and ran ahead. In front of the building, a dark-colored SUV sat in a no parking zone. Mario recognized the personized license plate.

Mario couldn't resist busting the man's chops standing outside the vehicle. He pointed out the red painted curb indicating a no parking zone.

A big bruiser of a guy with his arms locked gave Mario a look, unwelcoming. "I'm not parked. I'm waiting."

Truman met Mario at the top of the massive courthouse steps. A glance back at the brute of a guy showed his intimidation game was in full bloom. "He's a driver for the Savino family, a first-class asshole, as is his employer."

In the hallway, Mario and Truman crossed paths with

Lina Savino, escorted by a man on each side of her. In her traditional black dress, still mourning the death of her brother-in-law. Her piercing eyes would make most people feel uncomfortable. Mario just smiled.

"You killed Lorenzo and my nephew." Her expression oozed with hatred.

Mario nodded his head in agreement. "Yes, in self-defense."

She appeared to want to spit in his face—but didn't. "I wish your death to come as brutal as Lorenzo's."

"Is that a threat?"

"It's a wish—and hopefully will come true." The doors were held open by her escort, and they took a seat up front in the chamber.

Mario and Truman stood in the back of the courtroom. The judge, now seated, read through notes. On the left was Gilbert James, the district attorney, showing support for the legal representation for the prosecution. On the right was the defendant, Pete Gallo, and his attorney, Gustavo Martino. Half the law firm was present. Gustavo always believed in showing force in numbers.

The judge asked the lawyers to approach the bench. They chatted, then the judge announced a recess, and the two attorneys joined the judge in his chambers.

The room broke into rumbling with the absence of the judge and counsel. The judge had just taken his seat, looked through some notes, and took a recess; it was highly unusual.

Pete Gallo turned back to his aunt and gave a grin. Mario observed Little Pete looked way too confident. "This asshole cut a deal." Truman agreed.

The judge returned to the bench, and the attorneys went to their positions at the tables. It was hard to tell which attorney was happy with the meeting or tongue lashing the judge might have performed on one of them.

The judge spoke with somewhat of a disgusted look on his face. Judges rarely showed emotions, but he did. "Both parties agree to the terms of the plea?"

The attorneys responded, "Yes, Your Honor."

The judge hesitated, flipped over some papers, and closed a file folder. "The court agrees to the terms. No time served. Mr. Gallo, you're free to go." He slammed his gavel down. "Case dismissed."

After the celebration with his attorneys, Little Pete gave a wink of his eye and a pleasurable smile Mario's way.

"I'd like to put a bullet between his eyes," Mario mumbled.

Truman gave a side glance and pretended he didn't hear the threat.

Pete Gallo walked out of court a free man with only a slap on the wrist. Despite his connection to Lorenzo Savino, his criminal record, and day-to-day involvement in the family drug business.

Mario flipped Truman the keys and asked him to get the car. "I'll meet you out front. Take the umbrella too."

Mario interrupted District Attorney Gilbert James, who appeared to be satisfied with the results of the judge's decision. "We keep catching bad guys, and your office cut deals?"

"Easy, detective." Gilbert packed up his folders into a

leather briefcase. "Maybe if you hadn't killed Lorenzo and his banker, we'd have the leverage to lock them all up."

"Bullshit, his hotshot team of attorneys would have gotten them off." Mario was pushing the DA as far as he could without retaliation of a phone call to the chief. "I sleep better with Lorenzo dead and, who knows, on a sunny day, Pete might get hit by a lightning bolt."

Mario got out front in time to view Gustavo Martino grandstanding on the courthouse steps to the press. Lina and Pete stood proudly behind Gustavo, as he bolstered his client's innocence. Explaining the prosecutor encouraged a deal because it was a case he couldn't win. A settlement saved the DA's office the embarrassment of another loss. The Lorenzo family agreed so they could move on with their lives. His grandstanding ended, and the Savinos departed for their waiting car.

Mario caught up with Lina and pulled Pete by the arm. "This is far from over."

Lina rattled off something in Italian. "*Otterrai il tuo.*"

Pete smiled. "She said you'll get yours."

"You're threatening me? You're threatening a police officer?" Mario shouted as the car pulled from the curb. He took a deep breath. Slowly turned to see how many people saw and heard him act out. Luckily, reporters were busy on camera, making sure they'd get their lead story on film from the courthouse steps.

Mario spotted his car. Truman stopped at the corner for the traffic light, then slowly pulled forward when the light turned green. At the intersection of Broad and Tulane Avenues, Mario's unmarked police car blew up with

Truman inside. The sound of the explosion turned heads, and people screamed as flames shot fifty feet into the air. Cameras turned toward the tragedy. Mario rushed to the corner, although no one could get within thirty feet of the intense fire. Sirens were heard; help was on the way. Nothing could help Truman; he'd died a horrible death.

CHAPTER 7

THE CENTRAL BUSINESS DISTRICT fire station was half a mile from the courthouse. First to arrive were two fire trucks, and they foamed the street and had the fire under control quickly. Sirens were heard from a block away heading toward a horrific scene. The loud sounds of a deep horn blowing announced the arrival of the SWAT team as the bomb squad trucks drove up Broad Avenue and blocked the intersection.

News cameras on top of trucks tried to get the best view of the charred vehicle and possibly Truman's crisp body. Nothing made people tune into the nightly news more than a catastrophe, and reports gained bonuses for the best repulsive film coverage.

Barricades were set up one square block from the scene, then police crime scene tape was placed across the entire intersection.

The yellow tape was lifted for Chief Gretchen Parks's vehicle to come through. She parked a distance away, not to taint evidence. Mario rushed to her and explained it was Truman in the car. She ordered a full tent covering the crime scene to block any visual to the public. Things moved quickly, and within minutes, the only thing the cameras could record was the white tent and a crowd of thrill seekers.

"Did he hit something? Another car, a light pole, anything to make the car blow?" Chief Parks wanted the answer to be a massive auto accident and not a murder for hire on one of her detectives.

"No, chief. I saw it from the courthouse steps. The car blew up in the middle of the intersection." Mario bowed his head. "It was a bomb, and it was meant for me." He tried to hide his emotions, but the robust cop's legs were shaky. He took a seat on the curb; with tears in his eyes, he promised, "Chief, I'll get them all. Every last person who had a hand in this."

The chief, overcome with sorrow, could barely get the words out. "Get them in custody. The system will put them on death row."

Mario heard her speak, but his mind was in a fog. Deep in thought creating the list of people who wanted him dead. He'd plotted out his first few suspects in no particular order; the criteria, they wanted him dead. "Yeah, chief. You stick with the broken-down system." He wiped tears from his eyes with the back of his hand. "Truman was murdered. His wife will raise their kids alone. Their lives have been altered forever." He stood, brushed his pants, and straightened his shirt.

"Mario! Don't do anything stupid." She reached for his arm.

Mario pulled away. "This is a vendetta against me, and I'll handle it—my way."

She talked words of encouragement to the back of Mario's head as he walked away. There was no reasoning with him; he was in a zone and on a mission.

Mario spotted Howard across the street in a limo. A nod of the head pointed at the other side of the yellow crime scene tape, and they met in the back seat.

Howard wasted no time and detailed the half-dozen names of people so bold to put a hit out on Mario in broad daylight. They discussed the Colombia cartel but quickly ruled it out as the bombing suspect, at least for now the cartel wanted him alive. Dead, the cartel would never get its money.

Mario narrowed the list quickly to the Savino family. Lina, Little Pete, or even Joey, back in general population at Calabar Prison, were the most likely. Possibly the Russians? They had a botched attempt on Mario's life, after he left two of their best men dead in his apartment.

Mario looked closer at the list Howard held. "I don't see Julie Wong's name."

Howard gave a strange look. "Why would she want to kill you?"

Mario raised an eyebrow. "She's a professional, knows her way around a gun and knife. We've both seen her in action."

"I don't think explosives are her weapon of choice. Funny, you bring her up."

"Funny?" Mario's eyes widened. "Nothing is funny about that woman."

Howard folded the name list and slipped it into his pocket. "For now, let's handle the first problem."

"Cartel's money?" Mario rested against the seat, exhaling loudly.

Howard gave a wrinkled nose, half-ass smile. " As soon as the cartel gets its money back, it eliminates one group wanting you dead."

Mario sat silently watching the chaos out the window. His partner and friend of twenty years lay dead in what he could only imagine was unrecognizable body parts. His mind drifted to the early days when Truman was a skinny, young guy, ready to take on the world and build his career to the highest level, chief of police. He was well on his way to taking over his own squad when cut down by a bomb not meant for him.

"Until I made rank and was put in charge of the Eighth District, I'd only had two partners in my career." Mario's face was filled with sadness and he mumbled, "Now, both are dead."

Howard was surprised; he'd never heard Mario speak of his past partners. Howard knew little about Mario's personal life.

Mario went into the story, almost like he was talking to himself. Never looking up, he rambled about an earlier partner, fresh out of the academy. On the job, less than three months, randomly stopped at a corner convenience store to grab two sodas. Mario sat in the car, and when the partner walked through the door, he was hit with a shotgun blast at close range. He'd walked in on a robbery, and the robbers got spooked and blasted their way onto the street.

Mario saw the whole thing go down. It happened fast. He chased them into an alley. Caught them both ready to scale a fence. With their hands off their guns, he placed his to their backs and talked them off the wall. They threw the weapons down and turned around with their hands in the air. Mario broke a slight smile. The shooter said he didn't realize the man was a cop until after he fired. As if it made a difference—

Howard with his back to the door, engrossed as if he was overhearing a conversation in public. He hesitated to speak, but Mario had stopped talking midsentence. "What do you mean, as if it made a difference?"

"I don't know. It was so stupid for the guy to say." Mario's hands covered his face. "Like if he wasn't a cop or didn't have a uniform on, it was okay to point blank shoot someone."

"Did they get the chair?"

Mario's face buried deep into his hands. "Hell, no. One guy dove to the ground for his gun. I put two bullets in him. The other guy was the shooter. He stood, hands in the air, and I emptied my clip into his body."

A hand tapped on the glass and shocked Mario to the present time. He opened the window. The chief invited Mario to join her for a ride to Truman's house. The bombing was all over the news, and she had to contact his wife before Truman's name was leaked.

Mario mentioned Truman had small children.

"Their school was notified." The chief wrestled with her emotions. "Two female officers will pick the kids up and get them home. It's best we break the bad news to the wife and kids at the same time."

Mario stepped out the car. "Oh, my god. This part of the job never gets easier."

CHAPTER 8

THE NEXT MORNING, MARIO arrived at a riverfront warehouse, protected by an armed guard, a ten-foot barbed wire fence, and cameras. Military-grade surveillance with a live feed to a control room of all movement in and out was watched by a two-man team. If not invited, no one was getting in unless they dug under by tunnel or dropped from a helicopter, and even then they wouldn't get inside. It was called the large room. A twelve-thousand-square-foot open area where the FBI stored extensive evidence. Cars, boats, file cabinets, and most of all computers confiscated from organized crime, drug dealers, and serial killers.

Mario showed his badge and identification. The guard looked at a clipboard, checked Mario's name off a list, and the electric gate opened.

Mario parked his temporary police car in an area labeled visitors. He walked through another checkpoint and was escorted to a glass room. Given a face mask and plastic gloves, he entered.

"Good morning, chief," his voice muffled, like a sound heard in an alien movie. Twenty-four hours later, even with the mask, one could still smell the scorched vehicle. The car had been taken apart and labeled on the ground next to a camera on a tripod—everything was recorded. Three men in white coveralls did all the lifting, with another person at a high-top table on a computer. The only people Mario knew were the chief and Olivia, who perched herself over the woman at the table staring at a laptop.

Mario pulled the chief to the side. "This is my case." In a whisper. "Why is the FBI involved?"

"Don't get your panties in a ruffle, detective." She pulled him farther away from the group of workers. "The FBI wants the first crack at the car. I agreed. It has resources and talent we could never get. They want to identify the type of bomb, how it was detonated, and possible fingerprints."

"Rule out a terrorist?" Mario said.

"Now, we're on the same page." She pointed at Olivia sitting at the table. "She's learning from the best explosive engineer. It could help our department in the future."

The street scene took fourteen hours to investigate before the intersection was reopened. A black bag with "New Orleans Coroner's Office" in white letters stamped down the front of the zipper sat on the floor. Mario was sure it was Truman's remains found in the car but asked anyway. Unfortunately, he was correct when a technician responded.

"There, see this?" the woman at the computer said to Olivia.

Mario and the chief looked over their shoulders to get a peek. The engineer moved the mouse and circled around. "See that connection?" Then she switched to a split screen. "Now, that one. There is no doubt whoever made this bomb was in the United States military."

"I see the wire connection." Olivia noticed it was clean with a double loop; the other one was sloppy.

The engineer rolled the chair back and turned to the chief. "Either connection would have blown the car up, but your bomb was made by a person with experience, and the technique used is only taught by our government."

The chief pulled a seat closer. "Was there a timer?"

"No, I think they were cautious. Might not have wanted anyone else to get hurt. Definitely cell phone activated." The engineer pulled pictures from a street camera. "The bomber focused on the umbrella moving toward the car. Truman's face was hidden and with dark-tinted windows, the bomber couldn't tell who was driving."

Emotionally, Olivia still shook and added her thoughts. "Whoever did this focused on your car. When it crossed the intersection, the bomb was detonated."

The FBI wrapped up its investigation and promised to have a full report turned over to the Eighth District by the next day. A copy of the report, showing a military-built bomb and all the pictures, would be recorded and kept with the New Orleans FBI division. It was classified as a murder for hire.

The meeting broke, and Mario and Olivia walked out to the car together. Both were ready to investigate in different directions. Olivia with surveillance cameras around the intersection of Tulane and Broad, and Mario knocking on doors. Olivia agreed to handle the arrangements of a police funeral procession for their fallen brother in blue.

Olivia looked distracted. Mario thought it was the

aftershock of Truman's death. He was wrong. She asked to discuss something with Mario in private.

"Can it wait?" Mario reached his car and opened the door. "I've got a full day." He saw the tension in her face, her eyes appeared worrisome. "You okay?"

She nodded her head left to right. "No."

"We'll meet for dinner; Italian or Chinese?" Mario's favorite foods.

"Neither, my house at seven P.M. I'm cooking." The worriment in her face disappeared.

Mario agreed. It had been a long time since he had a home-cooked meal.

CHAPTER 9

MARIO ARRIVED AT OLIVIA'S house a few minutes early with a bottle of red wine in hand. He hoped it was the proper wine for the meal she'd prepared. He clipped a rose from her yard and knocked on the door.

When the door opened, "Wow" poured out of his mouth before he could catch himself.

Olivia looking different from what she wore at work. Her scrubs were replaced with a kelly green sundress, white pinstripes, and her red hair made the outfit pop. The final touch was an apron.

"Wine and a rose for the beautiful lady."

"Merlot will work." She peeked at the rose bush on the walkway. "And my favorite color rose—thank you."

They exchanged a casual kiss, and Mario took in a deep breath. "Smells like pasta with red sauce."

"It's about ready, finishing up the salad, and I have hot bread from Breads on Oak artisan bakers." Leading Mario to the kitchen, she handed him the wine opener and two long-stemmed glasses. "Make yourself useful."

Mario popped the cork. Poured wine for two and handed one to Olivia. "To a great dinner."

"I hope it holds up to your Italian tradition." The smell said the bread was ready to come out of the oven.

Mario looked around the house, seeing pictures of Olivia as a teenager, another with her mom in front of an oak tree on the campus of Tulane University. His mind wondered at the cozy home and thought it would be nice to settle down with the right woman and a charming little house. Olivia placed dinner on the dining room table. She smiled at him. It was all in front of him—one of the most caring women he'd ever met. She understood the challenges of police work, and to top it off, she was beautiful and could cook.

"Mario?" Olivia said, snapping him out of his daydream. "Take a seat."

He pulled her chair out, topped off her wine, and sat across from her.

No one could ever match his mother's red sauce, but Olivia's was close and way better than anything he could cook. They engaged in small talk, mostly about people at work, nothing about cases they were working. Both their jobs had daily stomach-turning events, not fitting for dinner talk.

Olivia finally broke the ice on what she wanted to discuss and what led to the dinner invitation. "I appreciate you taking the time to come over." She sipped the rest of her wine.

"A free meal with a beautiful woman." His heart was talking. "What fool would turn you down?"

She gathered the dishes with Mario's help and placed them in the sink, he split the balance of the wine between the glasses, and they sat on the sofa.

"I have perps in the box for questioning less nervous than you," Mario said. "What's going on?"

"Money," she said.

Mario wasn't thrilled about lending money. It was a sure way to lose a good friend. "How much do you need?"

"Nothing like that" was music to Mario's ears.

Olivia rambled jargon that made no sense.

Mario took her by the shoulders. "Calm down and spit it out."

Olivia walked Mario to a small desk and turned on her computer monitor. In preparation, she had her bank account opened on the screen. Strolling down, she pointed at the debit of thirty-two thousand dollars. Her face showed worry, and what was a fun evening turned sour quickly. She'd been to the bank and was told the money had been transferred by her. The transfer matched the IP address of her computer.

Mario's head, a little in a daze, asked, "Where did you transfer the money?"

"I didn't, that's the point." She explained that it was her investment account. The money went from the bank to her broker's account and back when she sold the stock.

"Like a day trader?"

"Yeah, I make good money jumping in and out of the market."

Mario tried to wrap his head around her problem. She confirmed her accounts were password protected, the money was debited from the bank but wasn't transferred to the investment account.

Mario was involved early in his career with a similar

case. An old couple thought they were ripped off when their bank account was short by twenty-five hundred dollars. The couple swore they never wrote a check for that amount. One visit to the bank manager cleared everything up. The husband wrote a check to the bank for a car note of two hundred and fifty dollars, or so he thought. It was actually written for twenty-five hundred dollars, and the difference prepaid future payments. The bad news was they were out the money, and the good news was they owed less on their car.

"Did the bank tell you where the money was transferred?"

Olivia, on the verge of tears, shook her head and handed him a piece of paper. It showed a routing number and an account number but no company name. Mario knocked back the rest of his wine.

"Who transferred the money? How did they do it on your computer? How did they get your password?" Mario hit Olivia with questions she had no answers to.

Mario looked at the day of the transfer; it had been two weeks before. She had done no transactions in a few weeks and that's why she hadn't discovered the money missing until now. Like a detective, Mario backtracked the last two weeks. Asking who had been in her house. She claimed no one, then corrected herself, saying her mother came by for a short visit.

"Gardener?" Mario asked.

"Yes, every Wednesday."

"Did he ask to use the bathroom or for some water? Do anything to distract you?"

Olivia shook her head. He cut the grass while she was at work. She seldom saw him and mailed a check once a month.

"Olivia, look at me," he said, turning her face. "Someone had to come in and know what they were looking for."

"How about a boyfriend?"

She made a face and shook her head left to right.

"A one-night stand?" Mario knew it was a personal question, but he was in cop mode.

She laughed. "Just you, and it was about two weeks ago."

He smiled. "And it's been too long." They laughed, and it broke the seriousness of the moment.

It was when her mind was relaxed that a thought came to her. "Louise—she cleans on Thursdays."

"While you're at work?"

"Yes." The woman had worked for her since she bought the house and had worked with her mother for years.

"Get Louise on the phone." He perked up, like he did when he got a break in a case.

"Now? It's late."

Mario persuaded Olivia. Louise answered on the second ring. When asked if anyone ever helped her clean, she replied that a woman from her church and sometimes her son would help. Olivia got the woman's name and address. Louise worried she'd done something wrong. Olivia assured her there was no problem and hung up.

"Now think, Olivia," Mario said. "Did Louise know about the account?"

"No way."

"Did you ever talk about money?" Mario dug hard for information.

"No, but . . ." Olivia paused. "My open mail sits on my desk. Someone could have seen the statement, but how could they get in the account?"

"I don't know." Mario ended the night. He left with the cleaning woman's information and concern that his friend had been ripped off. How? He didn't know.

Early the next morning before Truman's funeral, Mario visited the cleaning woman, Kathy Taylor. The woman was a church freak, and it showed when he entered the house. Mentioning Olivia's name got him a seat on her sofa. She was trusting, and it was scary how quickly she'd invite someone into her home. Even if she'd asked for ID, he wouldn't have shown his police badge; this wasn't official work.

Mario continued with a story that Louise had recommended her for a cleaning job. He zeroed in on her son, mentioning he understood she had help. Mario listened. Kathy gave up all the information needed. Her son worked part-time at a computer store and sometimes helped her. Now he was a full-time worker, and she assured Mario she'd handle cleaning by herself.

Mario quickly came back and praised the son as being good at computers for them to offer a full-time job. Kathy didn't let him down and proudly told Mario how her son, Logan, built his own computer at age thirteen.

Mario left her with hope, saying he'd work on a date for her to clean his condo. When asked where Logan worked, she didn't hesitate to reveal Bee's Computer Shop.

Truman's funeral wasn't for another hour, so Mario drove over to Bee's Computer Shop on North Broad Street. After talking to a few people, someone finally got Logan from the back, where he repaired computers.

Getting Logan away from other employees was hard with the busy showroom of customers. Mario spit out bullshit, telling Logan that his mother said he sometimes works on customers' computers at their homes. Mario stressed side work. Logan shook his head. He'd eon that when he was part-time. Mario had to laugh inside. Logan was as free with information as his mother was.

Mario gave him a sad story of an elderly friend locked out of his computer who needed help. When asked if that was something he could help with, Logan replied there wasn't a computer made he couldn't get into.

When Mario offered a hundred bucks for a service call and a hundred for the second hour, Logan couldn't resist. They agreed Logan would contact him the next day for a time and Mario's friend's name and address.

CHAPTER 10

THE PERFECT PLACE FOR Truman's service was Jacob Schoen & Son funeral home on Canal Street. It was packed with family and friends of Truman Burnett. The street had a line of police cars and a motorcycle caravan waiting to escort their fellow brother in blue to rest. Mario's eulogy spoke of a man he'd worked alongside for many years as a partner. He kept his composure getting through the ten-minute speech and his eyes from contacting Truman's wife or two children.

The procession was a short run to the cemetery on City Park Avenue at a family plot, overshadowed by a large oak tree making for a beautiful final resting place. The funeral ended with a priest speaking to Truman's wife, Charlotte, and kids. Followed by the mayor, the chief of police, and many officers who had touched Truman's life over the years. Mario stood under the oak tree, waiting for the crowd to disband.

The people dissipated, and the real pain of losing a husband and father was about to come crashing down on Truman's wife and kids. As the family loaded into two limousines, Mario approached Charlotte Burnett. Taking her hand, Mario promised he would not rest until the person responsible for Truman's death was brought to justice.

Charlotte appeared exhausted as she gave Mario a kiss, thanking him for all the kind words he'd said during his speech. Then the tears flowed, and she whispered, "You get this godawful person and make him pay."

As a soldier in war, there wasn't time to mourn. Bury your fellow comrade and continue fighting. Mario did the same—buried his partner and went to work catching bad guys.

Mario had an hour before Olivia's update on the bombing at the chief's office. He and Howard headed to pay Ralph Givens, their partner in crime, a visit. They met in the lobby of the investment firm at One Shell Square. The prestigious Poydras Street address gave credibility to any firm willing to pay the outrageous lease. Inside, there was a mixed bag of trusted people. Stockbrokers telling people where to put their money for the best return. The only catch—they made a commission when a stock was purchased and sold. They didn't care, as long as people kept buying and selling.

Ralph Givens went to grammar school with Mario, then lost contact when he moved away. Later, they met again at Loyola University when he was in finance and Mario was in criminal law. Ralph skirted a hair-stroke away from breaking the law a few times. Made tuition his last two years of college making loans to freshmen students. Blowing their money on girls and beer, they'd come to Ralph for a loan until parents sent a monthly living expense check. They paid Ralph the principal and shameful interest and a week later borrowed again. Things went well until a guy couldn't pay. Ralph got aggressive and knocked the fellow around. Mario stepped in and pursued forgiveness of the loan if the guy didn't press charges.

Howard ran a finger down the directory and found the investment company's suite number. They took the elevator, and to their surprise, the company occupied the entire floor. The receptionist directed them to Ralph's office, and they caught him off guard.

"What the hell are you two doing here?"

"We need to talk." Mario closed the door.

"We should have talked at a coffee shop." Ralph looked around to see if any office workers had eyes on him. "I can't have cops visit me at work. I handle a lot of money."

"No one knows we're cops." Howard buttoned his coat. Made sure his gun wasn't visible.

"Bullshit!" Ralph peeked through miniblinds at office workers. It was all in his head. They were too busy to be concerned who visited him. "What do you want that couldn't be discussed on the phone?"

Howard pushed Ralph into a desk chair. "We talked a few days ago. You said our money was safe."

Ralph squirmed in his seat. "It is."

"Then why is it not in the account?" Howard grabbed him by the necktie and made a fist.

"Your money is safe." Ralph made a fearful face. "I moved it to a mutual fund."

Howard gave a side look at Mario, not sure which man would use Ralph as a punching bag.

Ralph begged, then explained. He moved folders around on the desk and opened one. Pointing out the twelve million was accounted for in a mutual fund.

Howard exploded, wanting to know who gave him the authority to move the money. Ralph reminded them that when he set the account up in Singapore, someone had to be the administrator, so he named himself.

"Guys, I'm an investment banker. I can't let twelve million sit in an account and do nothing—I invested."

"It wasn't your money." Mario slammed his hand on the desk.

As a reminder, Ralph pointed out. "It's not your money either."

Things calmed down. Howard detailed the issues the money had brought on them. Ralph listened and studied them. The two detectives had concerns. What started as a scam to turn Lorenzo Savino on his Panama banker got two men killed and the money in Mario's hands. The detectives second-guessed their actions with no plan to return the money.

"Gentlemen." Ralph offered a simple solution. "This Helena woman is asking for the cartel money. Transfer the money back to the Savino family account."

Mario looked at Howard. They considered and mumbled that it would take the cartel off their backs and no need to explain to the boss why they took the money.

"With the return of the money—everyone is happy." Howard gave a side look at Mario.

"Except that problem with Julie Wong," Mario pointed out. "Well—two out of three ain't bad."

"One little problem." Ralph expressed a devious grin. "I can return the money taken, every penny. What do I do with the rest?"

The puzzled look on the two detectives' faces told Ralph they had no clue that he was about to make them both rich.

"The rest of the money?" Mario and Howard repeated.

"Yes." Ralph pulled a small calculator. "The market has been good." He punched in some numbers. "A little more than a million-and-a-half dollars profit."

It took a few seconds for the windfall of money to sink in, but when it did, they both had different reactions. Howard was thrilled the funds could be returned. Mario, the cautious one, wanted to slam a chair over Ralph's head. "What if the investment had lost a few million dollars?"

Ralph responded with his usual cocky attitude. "But it didn't."

"Holy shit, what have we done?" Mario paced the room.

Ralph soothed their concerns. Suggested they split the money, open separate investment accounts, and sit on the money for a few years. Estimated they could earn a hundred thousand a year if the market continued in an upward direction. He stressed, there was no law against borrowing money form a drug lord to invest in the market.

"Excluding the facts." Mario wanted to keep his voice down, but it didn't always work out that way. "The cartel didn't lend us the money; we stole Lorenzo's money. He was a mob guy who owed the cartel millions."

Howard nudged Mario. " We're millionaires." They both gave up a smile.

Ralph handled everything. The Savino portion of the money was transferred that day from the Singapore bank to the Savino's Panama account. An account for Mario and Howard opened with a little more than a million-and-a-half dollars. With the push of a button, all Lorenzo's money was back in place, as if it never left.

CHAPTER 11

EN ROUTE TO HEADQUARTERS, Mario got a phone call pushing the chief's meeting to five P.M. He and Howard headed to Roxy Blum's mid-city home. The drive over gave Mario time to fill Howard in on the plan to announce the discovery of Lorenzo's twelve million dollars. Howard agreed it might work.

Roxy was the lover of Glenn Macy, owner and publisher of *Big Easy Voice,* an underground newspaper. Roxy and Glenn would go to the end of the earths for Mario and Howard. The detectives kept Roxy's secret and helped skyrocket Glenn's *Big Easy Voice* subscriptions with exclusive stories no other newspapers had access to. Glenn and Roxy owed it all to Mario.

Roxy Blum, a drag queen nightclub singer on Bourbon Street, met Glenn Macy in the club one night. They fell in love, and, as the saying goes, it was history from that point forward. The only obstacle was Glenn's wife. It was still a work in progress living a double life.

Mario knocked on the front door. Howard looked over the immaculate garden leading to the front door. A rose garden with annuals edged the concrete and large, well-trimmed bushes were umbrellaed by a giant oak tree. One of many that lined Esplanade Avenue leading to the entrance of City Park.

"When the hell does someone get time for flowers?" Howard admired the front lawn.

"I'm sure there is a gardener involved." Mario knocked on the door again.

The door opened. "Oh, my god, where have you two been?" Roxy hugged them. "Come in—come in."

One in the afternoon was a little early to call on someone who worked till four or five in the morning. Roxy was dressed in a silk robe, slippers with fuzzy feathers at the toe and a slight heel, a wig, and full makeup.

Mario asked if she'd been to bed yet or was up early. She flipped her eyelashes, smiled, and changed the subject.

"There's my man." Roxy reaching for Glenn's hand when he entered the room dressed in black silk pajamas. Howard and Mario were outside their circle of friends but considered dear to the drama queen and her man. The detectives never judged their lifestyle and treated them respectfully.

"Have a seat in the dining room," Roxy insisted, pointing at chairs across from her and Glenn. "We're about to have lunch, and we have plenty."

Howard, genuinely interested in the art and antiques, looked around the room. "Is that new?" he asked, pointing at a piece of art.

"No, but it's a new frame." Roxy was impressed that Howard noticed something different about the picture.

"How about that fancy chair?"

"There, you see, Glenn. My new bargain caught Howard's eye." She gave Glenn a shake on his arm. "It's a Hitchcock chair."

"Yeah, you should see the price tag on what Roxy calls a bargain." Glenn frowned at the men, then smiled at Roxy.

Glenn broke the chitchat. "So, what brings you here? Hopefully no murders in the neighborhood."

"Nothing like that," Mario snapped back. "I come offering gifts."

"Last time you gave me a gift, my subscriptions jumped twenty-five percent." Glenn chuckled. "I'm listening."

Mario suggested Glenn take notes; he had a lot to say and wanted the article accurate. The headline would read "Mob Boss Savino's Money Found." Glenn blinked rapidly and reached for a pad and his phone.

"Have you laid out the front page yet?" he asked the person on the line. "Great; hold up. Save me two columns."

Mario put up three fingers and rolled his hand in a circle.

Glenn smiled. "Make that three columns and run an extra five thousand copies." Glenn turned back to Mario with pad and pen in hand.

Mario spoke nonstop without interruption. Glenn took notes fast, occasionally putting his hand up for Mario to slow down, not to miss any details.

Roxy poured coffee for everyone, and served a light dessert after a heavy lunch.

Glenn barely talked during the dessert and wrote, flipping pages back and forth on his pad.

Mario stopped the flipping back and forth by grabbing his hand. "How soon can the newspaper hit the streets?"

"Two hours and it will be there, front and center at the newsstands."

Howard gave Mario a nod and pulled his gun from under his coat and laid it on the table. "Glenn, this is serious. If your source is ever revealed . . ." Howard paused. "I would hate to do it, but you're dead."

Glenn and Roxy laughed until Mario said, "He's not joking."

The detectives thanked them for lunch and got a hug from Roxy.

A handshake from Glenn lasted longer than usual. "Trust is all I have in my business. My source for the story will never be revealed."

"Spread the word," Mario said. "It's your exclusive."

CHAPTER 12

MARIO DROPPED HOWARD AT his limousine. His priority was to collect several copies of the *Big Easy Voice*'s latest addition for the meeting with Chief Parks.

Mario headed back to One Shell Square. This time, he made a heads-up call to Ralph Givens. No need to surprise him twice in one day. On the way, he made a call to the chief. He got lucky, and she answered.

Chief Parks was hesitant to follow Mario's request to have the DEA join the evening briefing on Truman's bombing. The DEA had no jurisdiction, but Mario insisted, and she trusted her detective. A call was made to Commander Sanchez—he agreed to meet.

Mario bypassed the reception desk and went to Ralph's office. A coworker said he'd return in a second. Mario waited. Looking out of the floor-to-ceiling window, he looked on the St. Charles Avenue side to see a plot of ground he'd loved as a kid, Audubon Zoo. It was a once-a-year visit, his mother said, but he pestered enough to squeeze in two. As an adult, Mario still loved visiting the zoo, only it was hard to find the time.

Ralph came up from behind and startled him. "Looking to buy a house with your newfound money?"

"This neighborhood?" Mario smirked. "Too rich for my blood."

Ralph moved over to a conference table, where they sat. Mario spelled out a problem he didn't want to reveal in front of Howard. He detailed Olivia's situation.

Mario knew Ralph as a computer whiz going back to the early days of Microsoft. By the time home computers were widespread, he'd hacked into just about every model. That caused his first run-in with the law. Mario had kept him out of jail. Mario fished around and finally came out and asked if he was keen on today's computer technology

"Times have changed." Ralph snickered. "But I've kept up."

"I'm sure you have."

"For personal knowledge."

Mario laughed. "Until you had a use for it."

"Bank accounts are password protected. If I sit in front of a computer long enough, I'll get into every one of your friend Olivia's accounts."

Ralph suggested that maybe Olivia went out of town and someone housesat. Allowing them time to crack passwords.

Mario quickly shot that down. He shared his thoughts on a cleaning crew. The female-owned company passed Olivia's house off to a woman at her church. He detailed his visit with Logan at Bee's Computer Shop.

Ralph rolled his eyes, a slight smirk on his face. "Young, a college student working at a computer shop. I'd look at him first."

Mario wrote down the routing and account numbers of Olivia's bank account. Ralph questioned why the bank wouldn't help. All Mario knew was the bank said the money was transferred by using her IP address, ID code, and password. The bank was looking into it, but he didn't think it was a priority.

"If the guy is talented, he could tap into Olivia's computer remotely and make it look like it was her computer doing the transaction," Ralph tapped the table deep in thought. "I'll work on the IP address and see if I can find where her money is parked."

Mario shook his hand in gratitude. Ralph reminded him he'd just come into a lot of money and could cover the loss for his friend.

Mario made a face. "No, I want to catch this guy."

"Meaning the guy is in for an ass-kicking," Ralph pointed out.

Mario smiled. "Then justice would be served."

Mario departed with one task—to discover where Olivia kept her passwords and forward the info to Ralph. It could be kept in a Word document on her computer, in a notebook, or, like most people, just scribbled on pieces of paper. Even though he was on his way to a meeting Olivia would attend, he called her from the car.

Loaded with the information Olivia provided, Mario called Ralph after parking the car at police headquarters. Once inside the building, phone reception was sketchy. Olivia said she kept passwords to the computer logins and websites neatly written in a black notebook.

Ralph's theory was that the book was out in the open,

or the thief stumbled across it while cleaning. Either way, the guy didn't wake up that morning thinking he'd rob someone by computer transfer. He assured Mario the person had a background in computer science and a degree in fraud. He suggested that Mario check Logan Taylor for any arrests. Ralph confirmed it wouldn't take a computer science major to rip Olivia off, if the passwords were found.

Ralph thought the guy stumbled across the black book, found the ID code to an investment account, and checked out her transactions. Armed with access to the computer, the bank website, and the password, it wouldn't take much time to transfer money. With the homeowner's computer and black book of codes, she would never know she was ripped off—until she checked her account.

CHAPTER 13

AT THE HEAD OF the conference table sat Chief Parks, next was DEA Commander Sanchez, and on the other side was District Attorney Gilbert James, two FBI agents, Mayor Wallace Jackson, and his assistant Kory Barnes.

The mayor never left his office without Kory. If he didn't want to answer a question, he'd say Kory would check and get back with an answer. Which meant the mayor had no intention of agreeing and would say no over the phone in a few days. Kory never spoke out in a meeting or asked a direct question. Before the meeting started, Kory fetched bottled water and a cup of coffee for his boss, then took a seat behind him against the wall.

Mario greeted everyone, getting a sharp look from the chief. As if to say, "I got the DEA here; you better come through." He gave her a nod of assurance and prayed Howard would deliver.

Olivia entered the room with a look of horror on her face. Clearly not expecting so many people and top officials waiting for her update.

No call or text from Howard made Mario anxious. He

did his best to stall the meeting and lost the battle when the chief called on Olivia to start.

The lights were dimmed. Olivia started with a slide show of pictures from the bomb scene. Nothing Mario hadn't seen and studied for hours. She acknowledged the DEA and the FBI for the work they did in the investigation. Specified the FBI's assistance in finding the device that triggered the bomb. The slides ended, and the lights were turned brighter.

Mario's heart jumped a beat with a knock at the door. Howard peeked in. "Sorry I'm late." A blink of his eyes assured Mario he had the newspapers, and Howard took a seat.

Olivia continued and surprised Mario how far her investigation had progressed. She'd worked the VA Medical Center officials hard, and they came up with results. There were three men with military explosives background who came in for treatment. There were no physical addresses for any of them. A nurse described the condition of the men: dirty clothes and smelly. She suspected they were living on the streets. All three had military records but parts were sealed, so there was no way of knowing if they'd had honorable discharges.

DEA Commander Sanchez asked how the three men were picked out as possible suspects. Olivia thanked him and explained that the team narrowed it down to those men based on their military training. That much was available in their records. Two were born in the Midwest, and one was raised in New Orleans. All three were trained in defusing bombs, the type that blew up Truman. They were housed together and schooled at the same facility, then shipped to Afghanistan, sweeping hotels, taverns, and any place soldiers gathered when off duty.

"Surely if they could seek out and defuse a bomb . . ." Olivia paused and looked each person in the eyes. "They easily could build a bomb of the same type."

"But why?" the chief interrupted.

"Why? I don't know at this time," Olivia replied.

Mario recommended an undercover officer penetrate the homeless shelters. With pictures of the men, they shouldn't be hard to find. He volunteered himself.

"That might be a drastic move." Chief Parks shot Mario a look. "It's early in the game."

Mayor Jackson chimed in that too many roamers were spreading word about the explosion. He told his supporters, mostly preachers, that it was an isolated incident. His largest backer for the mayor's race was Pastor Ignatius Green. When he made a call, the mayor jumped. He disagreed with the undercover operation. Pounding the table, he stood. "I want my city back to normal. Am I clear?" Kory opened the door and he stormed out.

Side looks went around the table. The chief shook her head in disbelief. She and the mayor had not seen eye to eye since the day he took office.

Howard broke the tension. "I'll go undercover with Mario."

Olivia handed off the file to Mario, indicating her office was finished with its part of the investigation. Mario announced he'd put two detectives on the ground, while he and Howard lived the homeless life for a few days.

Everyone agreed except Commander Sanchez, who frankly said it wasn't a DEA issue and questioned why he was asked to attend the meeting.

Howard slid the newspapers to Mario as he stood. "Commander Sanchez, I'm reopening the Lorenzo Savino case."

"Why?" A confused look came over him. "He's dead. We found nothing, and Lina and Pete walked. Why embarrass us again?"

"To get even," Howard said with a snicker, giving Mario the cue to begin.

Mario did his pace around the conference room. "Who gets the trophy?" Questionable eyes focused on Mario's slang. "Lorenzo's money. That would be the trophy."

"Any money found in a drug-related bust goes to the DEA," Sanchez said. "The cartel snatched the money before we got the approval to seize Lorenzo's Panama bank account."

Mario tossed the newspapers across the table. Glenn did his part—producing the perfect headline. It read "Drug Lord's Money Found."

The chief and Sanchez reached for a newspaper. They were quiet, deep into reading the article Glenn wrote. Mario did a dry run of the bullshit story in his head. He had one shot at selling it and began with the publisher of the newspaper's statement.

Lorenzo met with Isaac Garza on the yacht the morning of the raid. Isaac was ordered to transfer most of the money in the Panama bank to offshore investments. The transfer had a timestamp of 120 business days, then automatically moved back to the Panama bank. Possibly to keep the money rolling in case the feds were watching.

"Today is one hundred and twenty days." Mario gave a glimpse to each person at the table. They bought the story.

"How does this publisher know?" Sanchez glanced at who wrote the article. "Glenn Macy, how did he get this information?"

Mario shrugged his shoulders. "The TV news picked up the story—it has to have some truth to it for them to stick their necks out."

Howard spoke up when the room went silent. "Check the Panama bank account." He pushed the routing and account numbers across the table.

The eerie silence worried Mario. Then DA James said, " I'll get a judge to sign off on seizing the account. Of course, if there is any money."

"No," Sanchez said. "This is a DEA case. If there is a substantial amount of money in the account, Lina Savino, an officer in the company, will have to produce tax records of its earning."

Mario gave a slight snicker and made eye contact with Howard. "Is twelve million dollars substantial?"

The DEA commander's eyes lit up. "More than enough."

CHAPTER 14

THERE WAS NO TIME wasted. Mario and Howard went undercover the next morning. Mario had an early call with the department's makeup artist. She created fake beards, mustaches, dreadlocks, and in this case, heavy gel in Mario's hair. Made it greasy looking, like a wash was needed a month ago. Makeup around his eyes gave a genuine dark circle effort, and she fitted him for raggedy overalls. Howard, Mario, and a shopping cart full of junk got loaded into a van. They parked on a side street near a busy intersection. Waiting for traffic to pass, including any passersby on foot, Howard gave the okay. Mario, with his props, jumped out the back on the vehicle, pushing his way to the corner.

"Shit!" Mario shouted. "Could have gotten me a grocery cart with good wheels."

"You're undercover—need to fit in among the homeless." Howard planned for a dreadful day. With a microphone taped to Mario's chest, he'd bitch at every little thing..

"Well, you're not pushing this piece of shit."

"Sorry, they were all out of new, smooth-rolling carts."

Mario moved the wagon of junk alongside an overpass. It was the perfect shelter area for the homeless. Overhead coverage, traffic for panhandling, and an interstate exit to the Central Business District. Fancy cars and people with jobs heading to the CBD. A textbook place to score some loose change as drivers sat desperately waiting for the traffic light to turn green.

Mario did his best not to make eye contact with the men and women who sat with their possessions in an area of the ground claimed by a line drawn in the dirt. He'd learned from his homeless snitches, they didn't like visual contact. Noticed enough to get a dollar or two, but deep down most were ashamed for the life they were forced to live. In makeshift beds and shelters made of cardboard boxes, they slept, ate, and watched when drivers threw cigarettes or half-eaten packages of snacks to the ground.

Mario thought he was prepared for the smell of urine, body odor, and spoiled food. He wasn't. The pungent aroma was strong.

"Hey," a guy shouted out. "How much for the blanket?"

Mario had spent little time looking over his inventory that the prop department stocked in the cart. On top, an oil-stained blanket had seen better days.

"Give me a buck," Mario shouted back.

The guy waved him off. "Too much."

"What are you offering?' Mario wanted to make a friend.

"Fifty cents," the guy said.

"Deal."

Mario took the money from the guy and let him grab

the nasty, stained blanket. "What's your name?" An attempt to strike up a conversation.

He halfheartedly answered, "Cyrus."

"Nod your head, if you're ready," Howard's voice came over Mario's earpiece.

Mario gave a nod and twenty feet away the van pulled into traffic.

"Nice to meet you, Cyrus," Mario said

The van startled Cyrus when it stopped at the curb. Mario assured Cyrus it was okay and he would protect him by stepping in front.

"Can I help you, sir?" Mario played his part and got aggressive with Howard.

"What are your names?"

"I'm Little John; this is Cyrus," Mario said.

Howard was holding his composure. They hadn't discussed an alias name. "Little John?"

"That's right, sir."

"But you're not so little."

Mario played along. "They call me LJ."

Howard played his part and stepped out of the van. He explained he was an off-duty cop working for an attorney. Flipped out three pictures, and Mario fetched the images so Cyrus could get a better look. Cyrus shook his head, his eyesight had long failed.

Howard rushed back to the van and returned with some reading glasses. Something he thought was crazy to request for their secret project, but Mario insisted. Candy bars, soap, and a stack of dollar bills too. He planned to spread them around for information.

"Here you go." Howard handed Cyrus a pair of two-and-a-half strength eyeglass readers.

Adjusting the glasses, Cyrus blinked a few times. "This middle guy." Then abruptly stopped. "He wanted for something?" Then returned the picture and the glasses.

Howard quickly reacted, pulling out an official-looking paper showing the three men in the picture were due money from a lawsuit settlement against the United States military.

"Really?" Cyrus looked closely. "The middle guy, I called him One-Arm Jack. I recognize the one on the left too." He pointed. "They are always together."

"When's the last time—" Mario said and stopped mid-sentence. His detective instincts had nearly taken over.

Howard continued the question. "When was the last time you saw them?"

Cyrus took his nasty Dixie Beer logo cap off. It looked as old as him. He scratched his long, greasy hair. "Maybe two days ago."

A candy bar and two bucks were given to Cyrus as a thank you. Mario put his hand out.

Howard made a face and handed him a candy bar, he kept his hand out for the money.

Then Howard handed out quarters. "Call my cell if you see these guys. Could be some money for finding them."

"Mr. lawyer man?" Cyrus gave a toothless smile. "When's the last time you saw a pay phone?"

Mario raised his shoulders. "He's right. Mr. Lawyer man, no street phones anymore."

Howard busted a big grin. Mario played the part too

well. He told them to stay put and by foot crossed at the corner and walked a half block to a Walgreens drugstore.

Mario buddied up to Cyrus. Put out a plan that two were better than one and if they found the guys, they could split the money. Mario pulled his shirt up showing a small revolver. Letting Cyrus know he'd protect him on the streets.

Howard returned with two cell phones with fifty paid minutes. Then he wrote his name and number on a piece of paper. "Call me if you see either of the men."

"The guy in the middle," Cyrus said. "I know him as One-Arm Jack but never said it to his face." He reached for the picture and showed how the man had his arm hidden behind a tree. "His left arm, elbow down is missing."

Howard gave Mario a side glance. "Good to know. The two on each end are Barry and Jay," he pointed. "The man without the arm is Leon."

Barry had hung with Leon for as long as Cyrus could remember. Jay joined them much later.

Mario wandered with Cyrus most of the morning and learned his history. He'd lived under the bridge for four years. When asked about family, last job, or kids, he'd shut down and Mario knew not to push. There is a breaking point with the unstable who take to the streets to live. It can't be by choice, and one had to gain trust before they opened up.

Mario parked his cart by Cyrus's claimed piece of ground and walked to Magazine Street. St. Andrew's offered lunch in the back of the church. That day red beans and rice, smoked sausage, and a three-day-old slice of Bunny Bread. Cyrus showed the way. Mario gained his trust asking easy nonpersonal questions. Cyrus told him where he could eat five days a week. Saturday and Sunday, they were on their own.

While standing in line, Cyrus gave off a weird look. "LJ, where have you been eating? I've never seen you around."

Mario's mind had a slow reaction. It was the first time he was called LJ. He'd planned a history of the last five years if asked—not traceable by a street person. His answer was that he'd been in jail for five years and was just released. Family disowned him. Broke and homeless, he took to the streets just a few days ago.

"What about the gun?"

"I stashed it before going to prison. The first thing I looked up when I got out of the halfway house. Not looking for trouble, but sometimes trouble just shows up."

Cyrus gave a look. Shook his head up and down. "What were you in for?"

Luckily the conversation was cut short when someone shouted. "Next!"

They got their plates of food and sat at a table. Mario scanned the people, looking for the three suspects. He saw a bunch of dirty men with heads down in their dishes eating fast. As if it was their last meal or maybe they hadn't had a meal in a while.

Mario ate along at a slower pace and monitored everyone in and out of the church hall. Howard's message came through Mario's earpiece, alerting him he was parked at the corner should he need help. A few words opened with "calling Little John" put a smile on both the detectives' faces. Mario covered his mouth and whispered expletives into the microphone.

Over lunch, Cyrus discussed a few places he'd seen One-Arm Jack during the day. His favorite was inside Lafayette Square, cooling down under an oak tree. Another was a bar he'd bum beers from, and a corner he hustled for cash. After lunch, they checked. There was no sign of One-Arm Jack.

They walked up Magazine Street and made a turn on Canal Street heading back to the camp when Cyrus stopped in his tracks. His eyes locked on a car coming toward them.

"Those two in the black Mercedes?" Cyrus kept focused on the car. "Some bad dudes."

"How so?" Mario said and repeated the license plate out loud a few times.

"Copy." Howard, down the street in the van, wrote the number down.

The man in the passenger seat stared Cyrus down. The car turned on Magazine Street.

"You have a run-in with those guys?"

"No, but Jack did."

"You mean Leon?"

"Yeah, man! Leon, One-Arm Jack, it's all the same person," Cyrus shouted.

"Wish I had a car." Mario talked with his chin down to his chest. "I'd follow the black Mercedes."

The Mercedes had just passed Howard's van. "I'm on it," came over Mario's earpiece. Howard picked up all Mario's clues. Cyrus was so engrossed with the Mercedes, he didn't think anything of Mario rattling off the license plate number.

By the next block, Cyrus calmed down, and Howard got him talking. It furthered the trust between the two.

Cyrus remembered the Mercedes with the same two guys pulling up under the bridge a week ago. Jack talked to them through the window when he and Barry got in the car and drove off. Before leaving, Jack asked Cyrus to look after his stuff, he'd be back in a few days. It was the last Cyrus saw of the two.

Howard's voice came over Mario's earpiece in a whisper. "Followed the Mercedes. Need your help. I'm on my way."

Working with a partner undercover, there were rules. Talk little over the radios. Even with an earpiece, the voice can travel beyond the ears. Get to the point and have a prearranged meeting place should one or the other need help.

Mario cut the conversation with Cyrus. Said he'd meet up later, then took to a side alley. He ripped the overalls off, ran a comb through his hair, and with a handkerchief wiped the makeup off the best he could. Like Clark Kent becoming Superman, Little John submerged from the dumpster as Mario the detective and ran to the rendezvous point.

CHAPTER 15

THREE RENDEZVOUS POINTS WERE planned. A two-man undercover team had to know their partner's location at all times. Mario had confidence Howard would head to the Fairmont New Orleans hotel, the Baronne Street entrance, as it was his closest rendezvous point.

Mario made small talk with the doorman, dressed in black tuxedo tails and a top hat, who stood on the red-carpet entrance of the elegant hotel. Mario's abrupt departure left the doorman talking to himself when Howard's van roared up to the curb.

"What's up?" Mario got in and they sped off.

Howard had followed the Mercedes to the Le Pavillon Hotel. The doorman remembered two men because they said they were from Florida, but both had Northern accents. The doorman was born and raised in New Jersey; he was sure they were from Jersey.

Like most hotels, the Mercedes was valet parked out front with other expensive cars to dress up the place.

Howard slipped the valet a twenty-dollar bill and his cell number. "Stall this asshole if he wants his car." The valet smiled and took the money. Howard called the license plate and VIN numbers into dispatch.

Inside, Mario bypassed several people at the front desk by flashing his badge and asked for the manager. A quick check of the Mercedes valet tag hanging from the mirror, and the hotel manager identified the owner as Michael Franklin by the driver's license copied at check-in.

Howard rushed into the hotel and found Mario. He'd heard from police dispatch.

"It's our guy," Howard said. "The license plate is stolen, but the VIN number is registered to Michael Ferrari."

Security led the way to the elevator, and they took it to the tenth floor. Security cleared the floor, having two maids move their carts from the hallway.

Mario and Howard approached the room number. A woman came out of a nearby room and all but fainted when she saw two men creeping with guns drawn. Howard quickly flashed his badge, and she ran to security at the end of the hall.

Mario, given a security keycard, slipped the plastic card into the lock, then gently pulled in and up. The light on top turned green, and he opened the door. Guns extended in one hand, with the other hand stabilized for accuracy, the two detectives entered the living room of the suite to no one. No voices, no showers running, and no TV sound. Michael Ferrari and his accomplice were gone.

"They left in a hurry," Mario said, grabbing pictures off the coffee table—of himself. Photos of Mario getting out his car, walking into the condo, even entering police headquarters. "He knew my every move, and yet Truman was the one killed."

A four-man hotel security team searched for Michael Ferrari. Restaurants, bars, common areas, and restrooms were checked. Surveillance cameras showed Michael and another man left the building through the loading dock, which led to an alley.

Howard and Mario rushed out front of the hotel, only to find the Mercedes was gone.

Valet man, cooling under an umbrella at the key box, got a finger in his face from Howard. "What happened to the Mercedes?"

"The black one? They're gone."

"I gave you twenty bucks to call me."

The valet handed Howard a twenty-dollar bill. "He paid me a hundred not to call."

The cocky grin set Howard off, and he reared back to knock the guy into tomorrow.

Mario held his arm back. "Not worth it, brother."

Howard snatched the twenty from his hand, then called dispatch and had an APB put out for the Mercedes. With the VIN number, cops would check every black Mercedes on the streets, even if the driver pulled the existing plate off.

Howard and Mario went back to Michael's room and taped it off as a crime scene. The more Mario viewed the pictures, the angrier he got. He pointed out that the time stamps on the photos were from two days ago, except for three images. The one of him entering the condo building, one talking to Jimmy the doorman in the lobby, and the third one of him entering the elevator were all dated a week ago.

"These are time stamped before Truman was killed," Mario said.

Howard checked the dates against notes he kept in a pad. "They were taken the day before your neighbor was killed."

"Could Truman's death and my neighbor's death be tied together?" A wrinkled forehead came over Mario, the look he'd give when he had a break in a case. "This is either the worse hitman ever or one unlucky person to mistake the target twice."

"Either way, he's our man," Howard said. "We have to find these assholes before some street cop does."

"Call home," a voice sounded in Howard's earpiece. Code when he's undercover to call the chief on her cell phone; he did.

"We're on it, chief." Howard ended her call.

"What's up?" Mario asked.

Howard pointed at the door and walked. "Chief wants us to check out two bodies found in Lafayette Square."

Mario followed. "In the middle of an undercover operation?"

"She said to get down there." Howard locked the hotel room door and added two strips of crime scene tape across the entry.

Lafayette Square was a few blocks away on St. Charles Avenue across the street from the former city hall. When they arrived, police had roped off the area, and a crowd of thrill seekers had formed.

The lead police officer met them at the entrance and walked Mario and Howard to the scene behind a bronze sculpture.

"A jogger discovered the man about an hour ago," the officer said. "Deeper into the bushes is another guy. Neither have identification."

Howard reached for the picture of the three homeless suspects he had in his coat pocket. Stepping through the brush, careful not to damage evidence, he matched the image against their cold, colorless faces. There was no second-guessing, the man with the prosthetic arm was Leon. He stepped slowly around the bushes to Mario. "This is why you couldn't find Leon and Barry."

"You're sure?" Mario asked, wanting a different answer. He wanted to be the one to put a bullet in Leon, convinced Leon was the bombmaker.

"Check for yourself." Mario waved him off.

Howard wrote in his notepad. One bullet in the forehead, each at close range. "Whoever is behind the bombing didn't want these two talking."

CHAPTER 16

HOWARD WAITED AT MARIO'S condo while he took a shower and slipped on some fresh clothes. On the sofa, he thumbed through some recent copies of *Brides Magazine,* why he wasn't sure.

"How long does Kate's subscription run on this magazine?" he shouted to Mario when the bedroom door opened. Kate was Mario's former fiancée. After nearly being killed by one of Mario's enemies, she called off the wedding and moved to Paris.

"Hopefully soon. I should have canceled it a year ago."

Mario fixed his tie in the mirror. "Let's go," he said, taking the magazine from Howard and dropping it in the trash can.

"I was reading." Howard made a funny face "Ten steps to make a honeymoon night to remember."

"That might be the reason you're not married. You need a magazine to tell you?" Mario put his earpiece in. "You ready?" Then pointed toward the door.

The elevator door opened, and the lobby button was pressed. Mario continued to count the reasons Howard wasn't married. They had a good laugh. A welcome distraction from the nightmares that had surrounded them in the last few days.

At the lobby, the elevator doors opened. They were greeted by Jimmy, the doorman.

"Detective?" He jovially giggled. "Did you see your cousin?"

"What are you talking about?"

Jimmy said he'd sent two men to Mario's floor just a minute ago. One man in a police uniform identified himself as Mario's cousin, Johnny DeLuca.

Mario felt the blood drain from his face. Then he looked at Howard. "I don't have a cousin on the job or by that name."

Mario jumped back into the elevator. Howard took the emergency stairs. Both were ready for whatever came their way.

At his floor, Mario stepped cautiously out of the elevator. He whispered into his mic for Howard. He was on the second-floor stairwell, opened the door and flagged Mario at the other end of the hallway. With guns drawn, they edged down the hall. The door he had just locked was kicked in and opened.

Mario motioned to Howard, and he went in first, low, with Mario over his head, their guns pointed. No one was in the living room. Scanning through the kitchen, they entered the bedroom together and quickly.

"Nothing," Mario said.

A sound from the back alley prompted Howard to peek over the balcony, "There they are," he shouted. "Unit five zero one."

They rushed down the two flights of stairs while shouting into the radio to dispatch. The police car and the uniform had to be stolen. Mario couldn't believe the possibility that another police officer would kill him.

Before they reached the lobby, dispatch had blasted over the radio to use caution when approaching patrol car 501. Driver wasn't a police officer but had a uniform. The doors to the lobby opened. They were greeted with a big smile from Jimmy as they rushed past him. In the van, they took to the back alley of the condo and followed to the first cross street. Police had the roads blocked. Mario flipped on and placed the blue flashing light on the dashboard and took the sidewalk, bypassing the police cars.

Passing the corner, Howard shouted, "Clear." And the same at the next block. Then retracted. "Stop!"

Mario slowly backed up while a police car with overhead lights flashing came up the street, moving slowly.

Howard reached for a pair of binoculars he'd brought along for their undercover sting. Aimed at the roof of the car approaching, he saw it was marked. "That's our man, car five zero one."

Mario floored the accelerator. Stopping sharply, he blocked the road. With guns drawn, they approached the vehicle. A man shouted with his hands out the rear window.

"Don't shoot. I'm a cop."

The rear door opened. A man with a white T-shirt and boxers stood. A gun was pointed at his head by a man in a police uniform.

"Put your guns down," the uniformed man shouted.

It was a standoff. Mario didn't recognize the guy with

the gun to the police officer's head. The driver slipped out of the seat with an automatic weapon. "Don't be a hero, Mario."

"Michael Ferrari, we finally meet," Mario said, then glanced at Howard. A return nod from right to left meant Howard didn't have a clear shot. There was no doubt Mario could put a bullet between the eyes of the man holding the police officer. But Michael, with an automatic, could gun them all down before they could get another shot off.

Mario tried to negotiate. "Any second backup will be here. Let him go."

The two gunmen shielded by the white T-shirt of the officer kept their guns pointed and made their way to Mario's van. The hostage was placed in the back seat, the gun barrel to his head. Michael got in and started the engine.

Slowly the vehicle backed out. Then faster, it took off down Magazine Street. Mario and Howard jumped into car 501 and took off in high pursuit. Mario drove while Howard called dispatch with an update. Not to shoot at car 501; real cops were driving. Mario was concerned that the entire takedown was so confusing he'd probably die from gunshots by his fellow men in blue.

The thugs took a hard left on Canal Street. Mario was a block away but coming up behind them fast. When car 501 passed a corner, a police car was right on his bumper. Two gunshots were fired. One bullet hit the trunk of car 501; the other blew out the rear left tire.

Howard immediately got on the radio to scream at dispatch. They made the turn on Canal Street on three good wheels. Sparks flew, and the gunshots stopped. They headed into a traffic jam. The thug's van was stopped in traffic. It pulled onto the sidewalk but had to return to the street to keep moving.

Howard and Mario left the car and took to the street on foot. With guns drawn, screams could be heard as they passed cars.

Mario made it around to the front of the thugs in the van. Pointing his gun at Michael through the windshield, he demanded for him to get out.

Over his earpiece, Howard's voice said, "On three." Then he counted slowly.

On three, Howard put one bullet in the head of the guy in the back seat holding the cop hostage. With both Mario and Howard's weapons pointed at Michael, they talked him out of the van.

"I'm throwing my gun out," Michael shouted.

"No," Mario yelled back. "Keep your hands high." Sirens rang out; police backup was near. "Hurry up."

Mario nodded at the cop in the back seat. "You okay?" He shook his head up and down. Then was told to get on the floorboard until Michael was handcuffed.

The van door opened. Michael stood, hands in the air, a gun tucked in his belt.

"Who ordered me dead?" Mario demanded.

Michael's unwillingness to answer pissed Mario off. "Who!" he shouted, stepping forward, finger on the trigger.

"My uncle, Roberto Ferrari. I can fix this between the two of you." He was down to pleading his case.

"Never met your uncle. Did you arrange the bomb?"

Michael spilled his guts quickly. Confessed to the death of Dale, Mario's neighbor, and repeated twice he had nothing to do with the bombing. Mario, a seasoned cop, knew too well that criminals would say anything to save their asses. Like killing his neighbor wasn't reason enough to fill him with bullets.

Mario gave Howard a side glance. Then he demanded that Michael pull his gun out from his waist. Michael reached, slowly pulling the weapon by the handle.

"Gun!" Mario shouted, and put two bullets into Michael's chest. He dropped to the ground with the gun in his hand. Howard fired twice, and Mario emptied his clip into Michael's motionless body.

Police backup arrived. Car brakes squealed. Cops swarmed the area with guns all pointed at a dead man in the street.

"You okay?" one cop asked.

"Fool went for his gun." Mario showed a slight grin. "He kept coming, had to unload my clip to stop him."

"I would have done the same," the officer said.

CHAPTER 17

Mario and Howard were separated immediately and driven to police headquarters. Standard procedure when police officers discharged their weapons, especially with two men dead.

The two seasoned detectives were no strangers to the process and took the time to mull over details during the drive. Two members of the police Ethics Squad were already positioned in each of the interrogation rooms when Mario and Howard arrived.

The Ethics Squad was trained to believe cops involved made a mistake in shooting, and it was their job to get the details before the news hit the streets.

Both detectives gave up their guns to ballistics at the scene. Olivia Johansson, the top forensic specialist, was ordered by Chief Gretchen Parks to oversee the incident.

The Ethics Squad personnel dressed in dark color, three-piece suits; white, heavy-starch shirts; blue ties; and red, white, and blue lapel pins. There were known to working cops as the Fashion Police.

The first process was for the detectives to turn over

their police badges, which both detectives had in their hands ready. It wasn't their first rodeo.

The usual process continued, as they asked both detectives to describe the incident in their own words, before they asked questions. A tape recorder on the table was rolling.

The detectives told the story from the time they were at Mario's condo. In their own words, the story came out the same. Questions were asked for hours, many the detectives were prepared for and the questions were asked several times with different approaches. Howard and Mario all but giggled at the interrogation, they had used the same strategies for years.

The cop who was taken hostage was also interviewed, and he praised Mario and Howard on the rescue. He said emphatically he didn't see the shooting. He was on the floorboard, crawling to get out of the rear passenger door of the van. They weren't satisfied and asked the question several more times, only to get the same answer. He was released and told to check in with the police psychiatrist for at least three sessions.

Mario and Howard were told to take a week off with pay while the case was investigated. The Fashion Police recommended they might want to check in with the police psychiatrist. They knew that this experience often had delayed reactions on people, and they might need to talk about it with a professional. They both declined, saying the shooting was justified and they would sleep fine.

With no police revolver, no badge, and no vehicle, the two detectives hitched a ride with a patrol car to the limousine barn.

Howard led the way to Ben Stein's office and unlocked a door that hadn't been opened since Ben's death. He motioned for Mario to follow him into a storage room packed with office supplies. Howard ran his hand over the top of a bookcase built into the wall. A beep sounded twice, and it clicked opened, large enough for them to walk through. A sensor-activated light illuminated stairs to a basement. At the bottom was a sizeable room with a bed, a full kitchen, a conference table, and a wall of guns.

Getting a closer view, Mario stepped forward. "Was Ben planning a war?"

"Ben was a businessman," Howard said. "Remember, one of his clients was Julie Wong."

"Shit, you'll need more firepower than this to take her down." Mario chuckled but wasn't joking; she's a tough woman.

A green canvas bag, placed at the bottom of each row of guns, made it easy to pack whatever was needed. Howard picked a few handguns, several clips of bullets, and broke down a high-powered rifle and scope to fit in the bag.

Back upstairs, Howard waved to employees working the call center for the limousine service, as the two men headed to the garage. The canvas bag went in the trunk of a clean town car.

A man touching up the windshield with spray mist flipped Howard the car keys. "Bring it back in one piece—please."

Howard smiled. "Can't guarantee."

CHAPTER 18

THE FIRST DAY OF the detectives' unplanned paid vacation, they compared notes of their testimonies given to the Fashion Police the day before. There was nothing contradictory said and both felt sure they would be back on the job by the weekend.

A call from Ralph earlier made Mario anxious. His first thought was to head over to Logan's work and beat him until he gave up Olivia's money. There was no doubt this kid was a mastermind with computer hacking, and no telling how many people he'd ripped off.

Olivia's money was found in an offshore account. Ralph traced the funds, but there was no way for Ralph to backdoor the program and gain access. It either couldn't be done or was way above Ralph's talent. He came up with an idea, and Mario was sure he could put it together. They just needed Logan to bite.

It was a little before noon, when Mario and Howard arrived at Riverside Inn. The men hadn't seen their old detective friend, Zack Nelson, in a few months. They went directly to the dining room and found Zack and Dave Thorton with their lady friends at their usual table.

A surprise visit was welcomed, and Emma Lou and Pearl Ann jumped to their feet to greet their favorite limousine driver and police officer.

"I hope you're here for breakfast and a visit and not come to recruit our boys for some police stakeout." Emma Lou still remembered the risk Zack put himself in by assisting Mario a year earlier.

A waiter saw the detectives and gave them hugs, then fetched two cups and poured coffee. The group had breakfast and talked about the good times and bad times they had been through together. It'd been two years since the last murder at the living quarters of Riverside Inn. About the same time Dr. Ross, who was responsible for the murders, went missing. The four men knew about his demise and kept all the details to themselves. It was best for the women, other residents, and police to think he'd skipped town for Las Vegas or some exotic island.

Zack, a retired cop of thirty years with the New Orleans Police Department, picked up on Mario glancing at his phone. "Waiting for a call?"

"Old man, do you ever stop working the job?" Mario asked playfully.

"Never."

Pearl Ann chimed in, making a wrinkled nose glance at Zack. "At the mall, he sits on a bench and points out shoplifters."

"You're an official mall snitch?" Howard got a round of laughs.

Mario's ringer was off on his phone, but when the face lit up, Logan's name appeared. He waved his hand for silence and took the call. Logan agreed to fix Mario's friend's computer. Directions and a time were set.

"Did he bite?" Howard asked.

"Like a largemouth bass."

"I know that look," Zack said. "I see mischief."

"No. Revenge." Mario's eyes glanced Zack's way. "You're getting your computer fixed at five P.M. today."

Zack smiled. "Great, if I owned one."

"You'll have a computer this afternoon."

Mario dialed Ralph's number and told him the plan was a go. He'd meet at his office in an hour and go over details. Ralph was confident he'd be finished setting up Zack's laptop by the time Mario arrived.

The details were discussed with Zack and Dave. The women listened carefully and were horrified how someone could take advantage of Olivia. The plan was simple, and Zack added a few things to the storyline, making it hard for Logan not to react to such an easy score.

Ralph met Mario and Howard in the lobby of his building. They parked themselves in the ground floor coffee shop. Howard fetched Ralph some lunch, while Ralph finished setting up the websites on Zack's computer.

While Ralph ate a sandwich, he went over the functions of the websites he'd set up. It had to have easy access, especially for someone Zack's age. The laptop opening page had several icons. Fox News, CNN, a dating site, and the most important, the homepage of the investment company he worked for, with Zack's fake account. It was loaded with 55,000 dollars taken from the detective's newfound investment capital—the profit from holding onto the Savino family funds.

Ralph started with opening the laptop, clicking on the investment site, and entering the ID number and password. One click, the account was open, and there sat Zack's money. If the scam worked, Logan would transfer some of or all the funds to his offshore account.

The ID was named something an old person would do in caps. "MY COMPUTER" and the password was "Emmalou72" his girlfriend's name and age.

"Here's the sting," Ralph said. "Zack will give the password to Ralph in all lower case. Making the site show a login error."

"You think it can be that easy?" Mario questioned if the high-tech kid would fall for such bullshit.

"Logan is a slimeball. He should be ready to take advantage of Zack, an old, incoherent guy in an assisted living facility, clueless about computers."

"It all depends on how good Zack can sell the con," Howard said.

Ralph gave a nod. "Correct. It's up to Zack to sell it."

At four P.M., Ralph opened the laptop to the guest Wi-Fi in Zack's room. A few practices and Zack assured everyone he was ready. The first thing done was to open the investment account and take a screenshot that was sent to Ralph's email address. Then he mirrored Zack's computer to watch everything happening, as he sat in Emma Lou's room down the hall. The screenshot was shown to Mario with a time stamp and a balance of fifty-five thousand dollars in Zack's fake account.

Mario licked his lips. "We just need this asshole to bite."

At five o'clock sharp, an announcement for Zack Nelson to come to the front desk blasted over the intercom. Ralph, Mario, and Howard took their places in Emma Lou's room.

Zack approached the front desk and met Logan with a handshake. Logan appeared to be a nice young man, asking questions as they walked.

"Got a little computer problem?" Logan asked.

"Yeah," Zack said. "I always have trouble with passwords. As long as I can login to my account, I love this internet stuff."

"I'm sure I can fix you up."

"I really appreciate your help," Zack slipped him a hundred-dollar bill. "I'm prepared to pay more should it take longer than an hour."

Logan gave a smile and a pat on Zack's back. "I'll take care of you. Don't worry."

Zack opened the door to his room and showed Logan the computer. "I'm trying to get into my investment account." Zack clicked on the icon and handed him a piece of paper with the ID and the password.

Logan typed in the password, and it quickly came back as an error in red letters. "Did you try to reset your password?"

Zack gave him a cross-eyed look. "How do you do that?"

Logan clicked on an email icon, and Zack's Gmail account opened.

"I'm going to finish my lunch," Zack said. "I'll be back in a few minutes, find my thirty-two, one?"

"What's that?" Logan asked.

"The balance in my account is thirty-two thousand, one hundred dollars," Zack pointed at a pad with the amount written down. "It's right there: thirty-two, one."

Logan gave him a smile and a nod. "Sure thing."

Zack left, pulling the door closed. Logan went to work on resetting the password. Within thirty seconds, an email came across, and a new password was set up. He typed in the information, and there it was, Zack's account.

From Ralph's computer in Emma Lou's room, the men watched Logan root through Zack's account.

"He's looking at entries," Ralph said, following the cursor on the screen. "Bingo. He stopped on the balance."

In Zack's room, Logan's eyes widened as he looked twice at the number on the pad, then back at the screen. "The old fart has no clue how much money is in the account," he whispered to himself.

Logan opened another window and typed in the website address to his offshore account, then typed the ID number and password into the popup boxes. He wrote "55,000" on a pad, then subtracted 32,100, and transferred 22,900 dollars to his account.

With a few strokes of the keys, Ralph captured the offshore account website, the ID, and the password. Without interfering with Zack's computer or Logan's illegal scheme.

In Emma Lou's room, Ralph rejoiced. "I have all the information to get into this asshole's offshore account."

Mario questioned. "Sure?"

"This kid is good but not in the same league as me," Ralph said. "I'm going to create a backdoor, grab his money, and never leave a footprint."

Mario made a face. "Not sure what that crap means, but if it gets Olivia's money, I'm in."

Logan erased the history on the laptop, including websites and passwords as Zack came back to the room. "Were you able to help me out?"

"Yes, sir," Logan politely spoke. He wrote the new password on the pad and took the piece he'd used to subtract the amount to leave in Zack's account. No clues left behind.

Zack tried the new password, and his account opened. "There's my money."

"All thirty-two thousand, one hundred dollars," Logan said, giving a side glance at Zack.

By the time Logan walked out the front door, another dilemma had come up. Ralph questioned if he should transfer only the amount taken from Zack and Olivia.

Mario looked at the screen. "This asshole has been at it for a while, he has over two

hundred thousand dollars in his offshore account." Mario's eyes rolled around deep in thought. "Leave one dollar. Like we did with Savino."

Howard chuckled with a side glance toward Mario. "It really pisses them off."

CHAPTER 19

BEFORE MARIO COULD CONTACT Olivia about the recovery of her money, she called him. Deep into the bomb investigation, she discovered something remarkable and refused to talk by phone. If they were going to meet, it had to be over food as they had all worked through lunch. They agreed on pizza, and the detectives were to meet at Olivia's home in one hour.

No quarreling about the order. These two detectives dined in, took out, or had delivered pizza from Venezia Restaurant on Carrollton Avenue.

The order was picked up, and they shot over to Olivia's house about three miles away. Olivia was home, and the dining room table was set with paper plates, a lot of napkins, and cold beer. All heads were into their pizza, when Mario broke the silence. "I have some good news."

"Me too," Olivia said. "Maybe more disturbing than good."

Mario went first and gave Olivia the news and a check from the brokerage account that Ralph had setup. A few guidelines were discussed. Deposit the money, change her bank password every thirty days, and keep her black book of ID codes under lock.

Olivia said she'd learned her lesson and was grateful for the return of the money but stopped short of asking how they recovered the money. "I prefer not to know how many laws were broken to get my money back. Thank you both."

They finished the pizza and moved to the living room with their beers. Olivia put on plastic gloves, the type she used at work. Opening her briefcase, she pulled out a plastic bag. Inside was a cell phone. "Everything found in Leon's pockets was sent to me at forensics."

She held the phone closer for Mario to observe. "It's one of those prepaid phones."

"He could have picked it up at any one of a hundred stores in town," Howard said.

"My concern is the pictures," Olivia said. She accessed the photos and widened a picture of Leon standing in Lafayette Square with Mayor Wallace Jackson.

"What the hell?" Mario said, getting a closer look.

She flipped to another picture. Wallace handed off something to Leon in a deceptive way. Both looking to see if anyone was watching.

Olivia's research showed that the first picture was taken two days before Truman's death and a second picture the day after his death. The second picture had the mayor pointing a finger into Leon's face. One could easily see it was an argument.

Howard's concern was who took the picture. Mario questioned how a snapshot was made so close. Olivia suggested someone had hidden with Leon's phone in the bushes. Based on the closeness and upward angle, it came from about eight feet away.

Mario questioned Olivia like a detective, asking why she thought the images were tied to Truman. She hit them with another bombshell. Leon's full name was Leon T. Mason, trained in explosives by the United States Army. He was also the half-brother of Mayor Wallace Jackson.

Mario's face drained. "You're sure?"

She nodded her head. Leon's Army clearance listed personal history. Olivia called an old military friend to access the records. Wallace's father died when he was eight. His mother remarried, and Leon was born two years later as Leon Mason.

Mario gave Olivia a sharp corner eye glance.

"You're not the only one with connections," she smiled.

Mario praised Olivia for an outstanding job. He had her text the pictures to his number, then she deleted the message she'd sent from the prepaid cell phone.

"Can you sit on this phone?" Mario asked. "Until we can sort things out?"

Olivia gave the perfect answer. "What phone?"

The question of who took the pictures and what the meeting was about were Mario's first thoughts. Did Barry take the pictures? He was dead, so he'd be no help. They could only hope the third member of the group, Jay, snapped the photos and could give them the answers.

Olivia flipped through the pictures again. "The mayor handing something off to Leon doesn't mean he killed anyone."

Mario's eyes rolled upward. "Leon and Barry, explosive experts, both are dead. With them out of the way, there are no witnesses to the bombing."

"Is it possible the mayor killed his own brother?" Olivia's frown showed she didn't want to believe it.

"It gives Mayor Wallace Jackson motive," Mario said. "So, he's a suspect."

That night Howard flopped at Mario's apartment, in case another attempt to take out Mario was planned. He slept on the sofa with one eye open most of the night, getting little sleep. Roberto Ferrari consumed his attention, making his mind speed with random thoughts of Roberto's next move. A man they'd never met had a contract out on Mario and probably Howard too. A long-running problem in the drug world, when one head of business was taken out, was that the chain of command up the ladder wanted revenge for shutting off the money supply.

Day two of Mario and Howard's break from work found them at Another Broken Egg Cafe having breakfast. Their conversation went wildly in different directions and always came back to how they were to handle Roberto Ferrari. It ended with the two men butting heads, Howard demanding he'd handle the problem, alone. Roberto, and any high-ranking soldier in the organization, would never bother them again. His words were convicting and to Mario showed a concern. The tone was emphatic without doubt or fear of consequence. Howard's motto was that of a real assassin—there had to be witnesses to be charged with a crime. Howard never left an eyewitness alive.

It had taken a year before Mario drew the lines between

the dots and put Howard on a rooftop, where he took out Jack with a single bullet to his head. With a SWAT team surrounding the house, Zack had been held hostage by Jack, a man who controlled the most dreaded gang in the city. Police moved too slowly for Howard's liking; he handled the situation himself.

Howard, on a rooftop, watched a SWAT team on hold while some commander tried to talk Jack out. Zack was already injected with enough juice in his veins to cause cardiac arrest. If it weren't for Howard, Zack would have been dead. One shot with a silencer on the end of his high-powered rifle ended the problem. He crept off the roof, down an alley. With the gun broken down and hidden, he passed the police barricades, got in his limo, and pulled away from the scene unnoticed.

Howard was never clear when discussing his background, especially with Mario. How was he recruited? In what way did Ben Stein and Chief Parks play a part in getting him into an undercover operation for the New Orleans Police Department? Fronted as a limo driver? A brilliant move, unexpected. One thing Mario knew for sure: Howard didn't come up through the ranks, because no one ever remembered him at the police academy or on foot patrol. He appeared one day as a limo driver with a diverse background from the United Kingdom, and next, he was working undercover. Stranger things had happened on the police force, so Mario never questioned when Howard was assigned to his investigation team. One thing he knew for sure: Howard would always have his back.

"Let's settle one score now," Howard said. "Give Adrianna a call."

Mario questioned the move. Telling Adrianna the cartel's money was back in the Savino family account could set off a war. Putting him in a mafia struggle to keep their money and the DEA wanting to seize the money.

"Eliminate one group of people who want you dead," Howard said. "Let the cartel, mafia, and DEA fight over the money."

Mario made the call to Adrianna; she wasn't happy. It was another obstacle to get to their money. She'd try to sell it to her boss, Helena Acosta. Mario didn't hesitate to throw his attitude in her face. Pointing out the money was in the same place as the day Lorenzo died, only a few weeks had passed. "Deal with it!" He hung up, which evidently pissed her off even more.

The breakfast ended with Mario contacting his new homeless friend, Cyrus, to seek out Jay, in hopes that he was the one taking the pictures of the mayor and Leon.

Howard planned to take advantage of the unexpected time off from work to visit friends. When Mario asked if his visit took him through New Jersey and a call on Roberto, he didn't answer.

CHAPTER 20

MARIO HAD NO PLANS to tell anyone at police headquarters regarding the meeting between the mayor and his brother until he had reliable proof that something illegal went down. Slipping money to a homeless guy, if money passed hands, wasn't a crime. Unless it was a payoff, and it was Mario that pushed that thought. Even then, he must be careful. The mayor had many friends on the police force and in city hall.

Mario drove to Canal Street and Claiborne Avenue, the start of the homeless tent city. A half a mile down was the fabulous French Quarter, where music played twenty-four hours a day, drinks flowed like New Year's Eve, and money exchanged hands like an open-air casino. How could the politicians of the city drive past this area every day and do nothing? The mayor, elected on the merit of cleaning up drugs and finding corporate sponsors to convert old warehouses into a walk-in clinic and housing for these people, didn't follow through with his promise, once elected.

Mario parked the town car and took to foot through the makeshift cardboard boxes these people called home.

He got lucky and found Cyrus pushing his cart up Canal Street, looking down at the sidewalk for money or something valuable.

Mario walked fast so he'd approach Cyrus head-on. One thing he'd learned quickly was not to come up behind the homeless. It took little to spook them and no telling what they might swing in defense.

Cyrus greeted him like they were old friends. Mario had treated him nicely for the short time they'd spent together. Dressed in jeans and a starched button-down collar shirt, he got a strange look from Cyrus. It was time for Mario to come clean. It took some convincing that as a cop he'd always be grateful for his help. Cyrus gave in and agreed to take a ride. As they drove, Cyrus had the air-conditioning vent blow into his face. Mario could only imagine living without air conditioning, and it wasn't even summer.

Not far away was Big Gabe's Car Wash. Gabe had an office and living quarters in an old shotgun house behind the retail business. Looking at Gabe, no one would ever guess he was worth a few million bucks. Why he hung around the business all day, no one knew. Mario walked Cyrus down an alleyway to the back door of the living quarters.

Gabe invited them in. Cyrus was reluctant, when seeing his size. People didn't call him Big Gabe for nothing, standing over six foot eight. No telling what he weighed.

"Is this the man you called about?" Gabe asked.

"Yes, sir." Mario gave a nod.

Gabe looked Cyrus over and made a call to the front office. Soon after, an employee came in with a clean logo shirt and gray cotton slacks, the same uniforms the car wash workers used. Given a plastic bag and shown the restroom, Cyrus stripped and threw out the bag with dirty clothes. An employee would wash and dry Cyrus's outfit, much like they did with rags from the car wash. The shower ran until the hot water ran out. Gabe shouted that Cyrus was welcome to use the razor, deodorant, and hair gel. Twenty minutes later, Cyrus surfaced with his hair combed, shaved, fresh clothes, and a smile. He admitted he'd not showered in a few weeks and that was during a rainstorm.

Gabe offered breakfast, and Cyrus wasn't shy. A meal at a table with real plates and forks was rare for him. Pancakes, eggs, and bacon were served, and they all ate.

A few times, Mario caught Gabe glancing at Cyrus. It was like he wanted to say something but was hesitant.

It's hard to relate or strike up a conversation. What do you talk about to a man living on the streets? How's your day going? What's living on the boulevard like? All type of questions you'd like to ask.

"How are the eggs?" Gabe finally said.

With a shift of his eyes, he said, "Good."

Cyrus ate slowly and used his napkin more often than necessary, maybe self-conscious of eating at a table with other people. One thing for sure, he was appreciative and polite.

Mario saw something he'd not noticed. Cyrus, cleaned up, looked like any Joe on the streets. He could have been in any business environment and been accepted. What was his story? Mario had to get him talking.

Gabe reached for the coffee pot. Poured coffee and

blurted out, "How long have you been living on the strccts?"

Cyrus's face showed surprise. Took a sip of coffee, brushed his lips with the napkin again. He didn't answer.

Gabe went into a story Mario had heard before, but every time Gabe told it, a little more was revealed. Gabe had a deep, alluring voice, it matched his size, and when he spoke, most listened. He got Cyrus's attention when he detailed how he and a friend came to the United States from an underdeveloped country. They had only fifty-two dollars between them. No matter how lousy it was living on the streets, eating out of garbage cans, and going without, it was far better than where they came from.

Cyrus finished his breakfast, glancing at Gabe a few times. He listened.

Gabe pushed harder, explaining that he felt Cyrus's pain. He added more to the story than Mario had ever heard. Before he came to the United States, he and his friend lived in a small, makeshift house. Their fathers built a tunnel under both houses that connected. Stored food and water for eight people. They knew the day would come, and it did, early on a Sunday morning. Rebels took over the village. Rapid gunfire got closer. His mother and his friend made it to the tunnel. His friend's parents and his father never made it down the ladder. They heard the guns blast through the house, room after room. They stayed down for twelve hours, and during the night escaped. Knowing there would be roadblocks leading out of town, the mother drove through farmlands and wooded areas until the car stalled. They went by foot, until a rebel spotted his mother and took her down with one bullet to her back.

Both Cyrus and Mario's eyes locked on every word Gabe said. He moved the dishes to the sink and continued. He and his friend walked for hours and were picked up by US Army Special Forces trying to take back the town. By the grace of God, they were helped onto a ship bound for the United States. The captain allowed them to hide in the cargo area. Ten days later, they arrived at the first stop—New Orleans. From the riverbank, they watched as containers of coffee were unloaded. They had no plan of survival.

Mario's eyes went from Gabe to Cyrus. His detective training told him that Gabe saw something in Cyrus that forced him to tell his painful story. One that left grief on his face fifty years later.

"As they say," Cyrus said, "the rest is history."

"Over time, my friend and I built several businesses." He paused. "We became wealthy, but not overnight. With hard work eventually."

"And your friend?"

"He died not too long ago," Gabe said. "His name was Ben Stein."

If there was a light breeze blowing, it would have knocked Mario to the floor. Gabe noticed his disbelief; it was written all over Mario's face.

Gabe, bewildered, looked at him to ask, "Howard never mentioned this story?"

"No, sir," Mario said. "Howard is a mysterious man."

"Yes, he is—he has his own demands."

The atmosphere changed. Cyrus looked relaxed. Gabe wasn't sure why after listening to such a heuristic story. He pushed no further in getting Cyrus to talk.

Gratitude was expressed for breakfast, the shower, and fresh clothes. When Cyrus spoke, it came from his heart. It seemed cleaning up took him out of his shell, to a point. Hearing Cyrus talk, Gabe noticed his vocabulary. He was far from the uneducated bum he appeared to be seen pushing a cart through the streets.

"Cyrus, what's your education?" Gabe asked out of the blue. Taking Cyrus by surprise and Mario too.

He hesitated—a long time. Then stood up, blinked his eyelids like he wanted to open up. "Why is my story so important?"

"Because I think, in some way, we're alike."

"Mr. Gabe." Cyrus's expression changed almost to tears. "I don't see how I'm in your category."

"Tell me something about yourself."

"I graduated from UL, University of Louisiana at Lafayette."

"Really?" Mario blurted out, surprised after seeing Cyrus's lifestyle.

"I was a high school Spanish teacher—five years."

Gabe demanded Cyrus to sit and begged for his story. He sat; there was a breakthrough. Like turning on a light switch, Cyrus pounded the table with his fist.

"My story is not—important!"

"Yes it is, and I can help." Gabe got him talking, and he would not let him stop.

Mario heard stories of his generosity—Gabe preferred

people not to know. A woman's husband was killed, leaving her with two small children. He'd send food to her house, found her a job, and made sure they had a Christmas tree with toys under it every year. That was Gabe, and now Mario knew why. He was giving back. He'd fought through hell and related to down-and-out people from no cause of their own.

Cyrus talked for a second or two; he didn't make sense at first. Asked for a bottle of water, which was quickly placed in front of him. As a child, he was abandoned, never adopted, lived with foster parents—many—until he was eighteen. Worked his way through college. On graduation day, he stood with his diploma on stage, knowing there was not one family member in the audience. As a top graduate, he got a job teaching Spanish and social studies for first- and second-year high school students. He fell in love and married a woman who also was a teacher. They bought a house. Made it home, chose their own paint colors, picked out furniture, planted a garden, and added a swing on the porch. They talked about the future. Life couldn't get any better. Then it did—his wife was pregnant.

Cyrus took a big gulp of water, it was apparent he was struggling. Gabe gave him a touch on the arm, and he plowed forward.

His wife didn't smoke, but he did. He promised he'd quit before the baby was born. The day of his wife's first doctor visit, he drove her. The doctor confirmed she was pregnant, and they would know the sex at the next visit.

On the way home, while stopped at a traffic light, Cyrus reached for a cigarette, to find an empty pack. The light turned green, and he pulled into a convenience store. The parking lot was small, so he double parked. His wife jumped out of the car and ran into the store to buy what Cyrus promised to be his last pack of cigarettes. She turned back and said, "the last pack, then you'll stop." She smiled, and he shouted back that he promised.

Seconds later, two gunshots were fired. A man ran out of the store. The owner quickly followed and shot the man dead on the sidewalk.

In the store, Cyrus's wife lay dead on the floor. The bullets the owner had fired inside the store missed his target and hit Cyrus's wife.

Tears flowed down his face. "I've never told anyone this story. Other than the police the day she died."

Gabe gave a few pats to his arm. "It's good to get it out."

Cyrus dabbed his tears. "I buried my wife and didn't leave home for months. I lost my job, the house, and ran through our savings. So, there you have my story."

Gabe fished around for the right words but there were none to ease the pain. He knew too well a person had to work through it or it would eat him up alive. It explained why Cyrus lived on the streets. He had nothing to live for. Gabe put his arm around Cyrus. "You have a family now. I'm going to help."

CHAPTER 21

WITH BREAKFAST UNDER HIS belt, a shower, and clean clothes, Cyrus sat in the front seat of Mario's town car a little differently than when he arrived at Big Gabe's place. He voiced how appreciative he was of Gabe's kindness for the third time, and pointed out it wouldn't have happened without Mario. It was hard for Cyrus to understand why he was plucked from all the people living on the streets and given a second chance. He'd stepped up and asked to buy Mario's blanket off the cart. The turn of events put him in a position to be offered a new start in life.

"You believe in the law of attraction?" Mario asked.

"I studied it and once believed. I gave up believing positive thoughts bring positive results and negative does the same."

"Why did you stop?"

"For years, I questioned that day. If the traffic light had been green, I would have zoomed past that corner store."

Mario finished the line. "And your wife wouldn't have gone into the convenience store for your cigarettes."

"Correct." Cyrus locked his eyes out the passenger window. "How did the law of attraction play out that day?"

Mario could only explain that Big Gabe popped into his head the night before, out of nowhere. Mario wondered why. Out of the blue, he'd remembered that Gabe had an old house he used as an office and Cyrus needed cleaning up. The rest went down unexpectedly.

Gabe reached out and provided Cyrus with what he immediately needed, food and a bath. Cyrus mentioned he taught Spanish and Gabe needed someone to manage his Spanish-speaking employees. Cyrus required living quarters. Gabe had a house he used for a few hours a day.

Mario had part of Cyrus's answer. "I can't say why the traffic light was red and why the store was being robbed at that precise moment." He paused and glanced at Cyrus. "Maybe the law of attraction didn't take you to Gabe."

"What do you mean?" Asking questions showed Cyrus had an interest.

"Maybe the law of attraction brought Gabe to you." Mario sat silently. A glance at Cyrus caught him smearing tears from his eyes.

Mario's cell phone rang, breaking the tense moment. The call from Chief Parks put Mario and Howard back on the streets as cops; they'd been reinstated. The chief had tried to contact Howard, but he wasn't picking up. Mario was to relay the message and both were ordered to the Savino compound on the North Shore. The Savino's money laundering account with millions of dollars was about to be seized. Lina Savino and Pete Gallo would be arrested, and this time the charges would stick. She was sure Mario and Howard would want to be part of the takedown.

Mario made a U-turn and headed back to the car wash.

"Cyrus, you're starting your job today." When they arrived, Cyrus thanked him for the fourth time. Mario gave him a salute. "I'll be in touch."

Mario headed to the Causeway Bridge for what usually took thirty-five minutes doing the speed limit. With sirens and lights flashing, he'd make it to Mandeville just shy of twenty-two minutes.

On the second try, Howard answered. He was delighted to be back on the job but told Mario to tell the chief he couldn't contact him. The story they landed on was that Howard went fishing. When Mario reminded Howard he didn't like fishing, he pointed out the chief didn't know that, so it should be an easy sell for Mario.

"Did I hear an airplane take off?" Mario asked.

"Possibly."

"Are you with Julie?"

"Possibly," Howard said. "It's like the military. You don't have clearance, so you're on a need-to-know basis." Then he disconnected the call.

Howard sat across from Julie on her jet, sipping champagne. "Where were we?" he asked.

"Something about taking out Roberto Ferrari," she said.

Mario drove at an excessive speed across the Causeway Bridge, much faster than the bridge police would have liked, even for an emergency. As a courtesy, they cleared the way so he could exit without a problem.

He arrived at the compound that was being protected by DEA agents and local police. He was expected and allowed through the gates. With all the police, FBI, and

DEA agents, one would have thought the president of the United States was inside.

Mario's car was still rolling when he got out. He rushed up the steps and saw a familiar face, Chief Parks. She should have been delighted but wasn't smiling.

"Get ready for a shitstorm," she said and kept walking.

Mario followed her to the car. "What the hell's going on?"

She lit a cigarette. She rarely smoked in public. Something had put her over the top. She took a few quick drags, then let loose.

The DEA had it all planned. They'd watched the money from headquarters, waiting for government approval to freeze the Savino family account and transfer the funds to the US Department of the Treasury. When the DEA finally got the okay—the money was gone.

Parks took a deep drag, then exhaled smoke up in the air. "Not a damn dollar left in the account!" She strolled in a circle. "No trace where the money was transferred."

She rattled on. Her career was on the line because of her trust in Mario. The DEA was all pumped up and had Washington, DC, expecting a big score and significant arrests.

The chief dropped her cigarette to the ground and twisted it into the dirt. "Here's the kicker." She stared Mario in the eyes. "I get all the agencies involved and rush over here to take down Lina Savino and Pete Gallo. Someone was going to jail, if not both of them."

Mario tried to keep step with the chief as she lit another cigarette. He had many questions, but for now he'd hold them to himself. It wouldn't take much for her to go bat shit crazy on him.

"You want the kicker?" she shouted again.

Mario nodded his head up and down, not sure whether to respond verbally in fear of setting her off.

"We stormed the house like soldiers at war. Found Lina Savino in the kitchen and Pete Gallo on the sofa. Dead—shot in the head. There's no drug money and no one to arrest."

CHAPTER 22

At 5:20 P.M., Julie Wong's private jet touched down at a small airport ten miles from the Boardwalk in Atlantic City. A place that families used to flock to in the summer for the long stretch of oceanfront beach, the Steel Pier carnival atmosphere, and food of all types. But it had long been replaced by casinos, crowded with adults, not only year-round but twenty-fours a day.

Evening traffic backed up on the main road leading to the hotels and casinos, so Julie's limousine took side streets to Roberto Ferrari's restaurant.

If anyone could get Howard close to Roberto, it was Julie. She'd been hired by him a few times; the latest to kill Mario but it was called off when his nephew, Michael, begged for a second chance.

They were met at the front entrance by a flashily dressed hostess. Whatever Julie whispered in the sexy lady's ear opened a path led by two strong arms to Roberto Ferrari. Howard's eyes roamed the busy place. It was early evening, and the place was packed with well-dressed customers, probably having early dinner before catching a headliner show at a casino. Whatever the reason, most restaurants would kill for this much business at this time of day.

Before getting to the glass room that surrounded Roberto, Julie's purse was taken from her, and Howard was routed to the kitchen by the two men.

"What's the problem?" Howard allowed the guy to remove his coat. "Be careful, that jacket cost more than you make in a week." His attitude changed from the "don't give a crap" cop to the assassin he was known as in the underground world of two foreign countries.

He would soon be introduced to the man who ran the East Coast and collected money from all the bosses he empowered, building his wealth along the way.

"My name is Sal," one guy identified himself. "No one has a sit-down with the boss without being frisked."

Howard held his hands up, as one goon frisked him thoroughly for a weapon, then walked into Mr. Ferrari's private room at the rear of the restaurant.

Julie had described the glass-enclosed room perfectly. Bullet-resistant glass was six feet high and double-paned to the ceiling. Roberto was well under six feet tall, so when he stood, no part of his body was in the line of fire. Should someone try to take him out. Too bad for anyone taller.

Howard could only guess that the man at the table dressed in a suit and tie was Roberto. He was arrested at twenty-two, and there was only one picture found in the police database.

They talked about the weather, the flight, the traffic, and other uninteresting topics as an icebreaker. It gave Howard time to look over his opponents, should things get out of hand. Sitting next to Roberto was Bobby G., just like Julie said he would be. The two goons stood at the door inside the room, different from what Julie said. They were usually positioned outside the area with eyes on who came in the front door.

Howard offered his condolences on the death of Roberto's nephew, Michael. A lid was put on Michael's death in New Orleans. All that hit the papers was that he died in a shootout with police. Roberto's reaction to Howard's comforting words wasn't expected.

"Sooner or later, he was going to get himself killed." Roberto wrinkled his nose. "As far as I'm concerned, it didn't come soon enough. Kids been a screw up all his life."

Roberto, a cold-blooded killer, had no time for feelings or family. "So, why did you request a sit-down, Mr. Blitz?"

Howard watched the two goons from the corner of his eye. They widened out a little and were three feet to each side of him, maybe four steps back, he estimated. "I need a favor."

"If you have the money, I can grant anything."

"Call the contract off on Mario DeLuca." Howard shot him a deep frown that made Roberto uncomfortable.

"Don't know what you're talking about."

Howard drilled him, taking a big chance if he was wrong. Revealed he knew about the guy and his girlfriend dead in the wrong apartment. The bomb that killed the wrong cop.

Roberto's emotion changed, his cheeks a little red, his eyes piercing. "Jul . . . ie!" He stretched out her name.

"Don't look at me." Julie quickly took the defense. "This guy knows more about your business than me."

"How come I couldn't find any info on this—Howard Blitz?" Roberto pointed at Julie, his face redder by the second.

Howard's name was well-hidden on the police roster, with years of undercover work. One would never find records of him on the city payroll, no such person as Howard Blitz.

Roberto motioned to Sal. "Was he checked?"

"Yes, boss."

"Recheck him." Julie was right again. He could blow up without warning. "Gun, recorder, whatever's in his pockets."

Sal grabbed Howard by the underarms and stood him up.

With one swift movement, Howard ripped Sal's gun from his shoulder holster and kicked the other guy, knocking him to the floor. "I've already been frisked," he said, circling the gun from Sal to Bobby G., then Roberto. The surprised look couldn't be described by any of them; not even Julie expected Howard's reaction.

"I'm a cop! Dirty, but still a cop," Howard said. Then he emptied the gun, dropping the bullets into his coat pocket, and placed the weapon on the table and sat down.

Roberto's heart rate elevated to the point he could hardly speak. "What the hell do you want?"

"Boss, let me take him out back," Sal said.

"Please," Howard said. "Don't make that mistake. I've come to talk."

Roberto motioned for the bodyguards to stand post outside the glass wall. "Find me two bodyguards who can actually protect me," he said with a shoulder toward Bobby G.

Howard explained that Roberto was interfering with his job to take out Mario DeLuca. When asked who hired Howard, he didn't provide an answer. It was too early to spill his lies. He needed more from Roberto, holding back might keep him talking.

"Why do so many people want this Mario guy dead?" He raised a bottle from the table. "Wine?" Howard accepted the gesture and it showed a calmer Roberto.

Howard fed him a tidbit. "He's in the way."

"He's got a big mouth too," Roberto said. "Aside from killing one of my best earners."

"Lorenzo Savino?" Howard asked, then took a sip of wine.

Roberto didn't answer, his eyes said he wanted to tell more. Howard pushed harder. "You think Mario did it alone?"

The room was silent. Howard glanced at Julie; she didn't make eye contact.

Then Roberto spoke. "My sources say it was Mario DeLuca, and some lady cop, Olivia, helped."

Howard was sure that Roberto had never seen his face. Roberto believing that Mario and Olivia acted to kill Lorenzo meant Chief Parks had done her job in keeping his name out of the killing. "Why say he's a big mouth?"

A sharp side angle look came from Julie, maybe he was pushing too hard.

Roberto raised the empty wine bottle to a waiter outside the glass room. Within seconds, a new bottle was placed on the table. He mulled around and then poured some wine, fixed his napkin.

Come on, asshole. Tell me why Mario is a big mouth. Howard was sure he was ready to give it up. Bosses love to brag on their accomplishments of illegal activity.

There was something other than Mario taking out Lorenzo that had Roberto so pissed. Stopping the mafia's money stream could kill anyone, but Howard smelled more.

"Why do you want Mario dead?" Roberto asked again, staring Howard down like they were in a high-stake poker game. He was trying to read Howard, but that would never happen. He was a stone professional. If there were college classes for assassins, he would have graduated with honors and top of his class.

Howard was well-prepared and had his story ready, expecting the question. A year ago a businessman, who issued hospital certificates, was introduced to the governor of Louisiana. It's what developers needed to build a hospital. The certificate was worth three times the cost of the building. The businessman had permits in several cities. Before the hospital broke ground, the paperwork switched hands, and the businessman walked away with millions of dollars for doing nothing.

Somehow, Mario, at some state police luncheon, got on the governor's ear and the next day, the company's hospital certificate was pulled.

Howard had done his homework. There was such a deal between a man and the governor; it was in the paper a few months back. The deal fell through, because the governor didn't think the first guy was a good fit for the city of New Orleans. Mario had no involvement, but there was no way Roberto could dispute the point.

"I set up the meeting with the governor and was due a million dollars if the deal went through," Howard said. "Is that not grounds to kill the asshole?"

Roberto smiled. It was a good sign, and Howard used it to his advantage. "A million bucks might be funny to some, but to me it's a lot of money."

"Don't get too excited," Roberto said. "I can top that."

Bobby G., who had yet to say a word, reached for his boss's arm. "Hold up, boss."

Roberto pulled away, waving him off. It was nothing more than what the newspaper and TV reported. He jumped around, talking about his investments in Atlantic City casinos, not in gambling because a license was required and a background check he'd never pass. His investments were in paper products, food supply (mostly poultry and ground beef), and coffee.

Louisiana, with one land-based casino, was ready to vote on riverboat gambling. It was a shoo-in to be approved. All that was left was for the mayor to issue the license to the many qualified companies that applied. Roberto's company was ready to roll into the Crescent City and take over the food supply business, just like he'd done on the East Coast. Vendors were bought out at unwilling prices, others' trucks got hijacked on delivery until they finally gave up and closed shop.

Howard listened carefully, and before Roberto

finished, he had the answer why Mario became a target. At a town meeting at a French Quarter hotel ballroom, restaurant managers, retail merchants, hotel managers, and even some owners were present. The media flocked around the place as Mario spoke about what came with casinos. He discussed traffic into the CBD and that French Quarter that would look like New Year's Eve or Mardi Gras every day. Street crime would rise; people would have less discretionary income to eat out at restaurants or go shopping. Hotels would gain from the casinos, until the casinos built their own hotels and gave rooms away to high rollers. People who spent thousands of dollars a night on suites in French Quarter hotels would then get complimentary rooms, food, and all the alcohol they could consume.

Mario painted a gloomy picture for merchants, especially for restaurants, bars, and hotels, which made up the majority of the businesses affected if casinos came to the city. Residents protested the casinos, and the media ran with Mario's view to vote down gambling. Other publishers picked up on the negatives of riverboat casino gambling. Traffic influx into the neighborhood would become main roads where bumper-to-bumper cars would damage streets.

"This big mouth started a snowball rolling downhill," Roberto said.

Howard took a shot to see if he'd bite and asked an off-the-wall question. "Who's working on the ground?"

Roberto gave a confused look.

"Who's looking out for your interests? Eyes and ears

on the streets of New Orleans?" Howard asked, watching for a reaction. "I'm available, have connections with the city council and police headquarters."

Roberto smiled. "I have all the boots I need on the ground. Mayor Wallace Jackson, soon to be reelected, has a lot to gain if gambling is approved. I should say when it's approved."

Howard watched Bobby G's face. It told the story that the mayor was the player on the ground, and it shouldn't have been leaked. Roberto was too concerned with impressing Howard, as if there was a winner for more connections with the city powers. Roberto couldn't resist revealing that he had the number one man at city hall in his pocket.

In the end, Roberto admitted to two missed attacks on Mario. He agreed to call off the hit—for thirty days.

Howard threw in a bonus. He'd kill Olivia when he took out Mario as a thank you for cooperating. The plan went perfectly. Howard bought time for Mario and Olivia, while he worked on taking down Roberto and his crew.

"Mr. Blitz, let me be clear." Roberto stopped him before he got to the door. "Thirty days to take out these cops."

"No problem, sir."

Julie gave Roberto a kiss on the cheek. "It'll work out."

"One more thing." Roberto, a stone-cold psychopath's attitude changed, and his face was now beet red. "Ever attempt to muscle my people or threaten me again—I'll kill you myself."

Howard took the gun and walked. Julie followed. At the door, he flipped the empty weapon to the bodyguard.

"Want me dead?" Howard broke a smile. "Better bring more than these two goons—a lot more."

CHAPTER 23

HOWARD'S EARS VIBRATED, NOT from the loudness of jet engines when he walked off the airplane but from Julie's voice. She'd preached to him the entire flight back to New Orleans. She demanded an explanation of his actions with Roberto. People just didn't talk to a mafia boss in such a way. Condescending talk to a man with power, money, and no conscience was a way to get killed.

Howard, happy the way the meeting went, assured Julie she'd overreacted. He thanked her for the introduction to Roberto. If another sit-down was required, he'd arrange it with Bobby G. directly.

Howard asked her for one more favor. Her frustration showed. "What?"

"Call me if you get another job from Roberto."

"Tell you if I get a contract job?" She laughed. "Why? So I can get arrested?"

"I'll always be indebted to you," Howard said. "I promise, and Mario too, we'll do whatever it takes to keep you from being arrested. Unless you try to kill one of us."

"Fair enough." She watched his car pull away and mumbled. "That's one crazy bastard."

Before hitting the highway, Howard checked his calls. It was the first time he'd seen so many messages. Usually he was prompt at returning calls, but under the circumstances he wasn't free to talk in the presence of Roberto and wasn't answering any on the plane with Julie listening. From one assassin to another, they kept each other at arm's length. Mario and Olivia left one unnerving message after another.

He called Mario first, and he picked up on the second ring.

"Where the hell have you been?"

"Saving your ass," Howard said. "What's up?"

Mario played it off casually and rattled off that the money sent back to Savino's account was missing, Lina and Little Pete were dead, and he and Cyrus found Jay.

"And remember that we've been reinstated," he said. "Pick up your gun and your shield."

They agreed to meet at Liuzza by the Track, a mid-city grill they both favored.

Howard arrived first and got a table for two, away from the noisy bar area. That was quickly changed to a table for four when Mario walked in with Olivia and Cyrus. He welcomed them with a smile, only to get a sharp frown from Olivia.

"Holy crap." Howard smiled with open arms. "Cyrus cleans up good."

"Yes, thanks to the both of you," he said. "I've got a job too."

Howard gave Mario a glance. "A long story." Then rolled his eyes.

"I've got to go," Cyrus said. "My ride is waiting. I just wanted to thank you both in person for all your kindness."

Once Cyrus departed, everyone was ready to speak out and put all the pieces of the puzzle together. Lunch was ordered and served with sweet tea, and the conversation stopped for a few seconds to eat.

Howard filled them in on the details of his meeting with Roberto. Olivia was horrified that she was a target with a thirty-day clock ticking. She asked how he got a sit-down with a mafia kingpin like Roberto. Howard was tight-lipped, and Mario truthfully had no idea, although the jet engines when they talked on the phone indicated that Julie might be involved.

Olivia pointed out she had proof to go to the DA. Leon's fingerprints were found on the chassis of the car, and she found a tiny one on a wire the FBI said came from the bomb. With Leon having only one hand, he must have had to use a finger and a thumb to attach the wires.

Howard suggested it might be a move to consider. Push the district attorney to close the case. The bomber was dead; who killed him was an entirely different investigation.

Mario's eyes looked at the ceiling, then made some rolling motions. "Might be the right play while we go after the mayor."

"I have one other nugget of information," Howard said. "Mayor Wallace Jackson is on Roberto's payroll."

Mario and Olivia were lost for words. When asked if he was sure, Howard clarified there was no doubt. It was Roberto who wanted Mario dead for his speech to the city council against New Orleans legalizing riverboat gambling casinos—and for killing Lorenzo, one of his best earners.

"Does he know we killed Michael?" Mario asked.

"No," Howard said. "He was pleased to know Michael was dead. Didn't care who killed him."

Mario brought them up to date on locating Jay. It would have never happened without the help of Cyrus. Jay, placed in a holding tank, wasn't charged with anything and would have to be released within twelve hours. He admitted taking pictures of Leon and Wallace. Money exchanged hands between them, because Jay was paid two hundred dollars from the very envelope Wallace handed off to Leon.

"A lot of money for taking a picture," Olivia said.

Mario smiled. "A couple of bucks extra for hiding in the bushes."

Jay was paid to take the pictures as proof of Leon meeting with the mayor. Jay was told it was a precaution, and Leon hoped he'd never need them. Mario pressured him hard about the bomb and was convinced that Jay wasn't involved and knew nothing about the act.

Cyrus found Jay at a bar on the corner of Bourbon and Conti Streets. This time, Jay wasn't hustling people out front; he was on a bar stool inside. It was a change of life for a homeless guy. All cleaned up, shaved, and a fresh haircut with a twenty-dollar bill on the counter and several empty glasses. He'd been there awhile, Cyrus told Mario.

Jay invested the two hundred dollars for picture taking in himself. He'd just returned from a job interview and was hired at a local grocery store—stocking shelves. He was at the bar celebrating.

"So why did Jay take pictures of Leon and the mayor's brother?" Olivia questioned.

"Proof, if needed as a payoff for building the bomb," Howard said. "In case Leon got caught. Wallace would have to help him with his political power, or Leon would implicate the mayor."

"The mayor had his own plan." Mario gave a mysterious look. "Leave no witnesses."

The table went silent, and Olivia took that opportunity to leave and promised to keep them in the loop.

Mario and Howard paid the bill and headed to Central Lockup to combine their efforts to squeeze more information out of Jay, if he had any to give.

Police headquarters was a block away from Central Lockup. It gave Howard time to play nice with the chief and accept her formal greetings of his reinstatement.

Handing over his badge and his weapon, Chief Parks gave him a piercing expression. "Try not to kill anyone this week."

Howard smiled. "I'll do my best."

At Central Lockup, the detectives waited for Jay to be brought down to the questioning room. A word from the sergeant on duty was to the point. Charge Jay or cut him loose; he needed the cell. No need to hold him if he would be released in a few hours.

In the room, Jay sat across from Mario while Howard stood. He wasn't cuffed, and the men offered a Coke, which he accepted.

Mario played nice, telling him he could go, but he had a few more questions he might answer to help solve Leon and Barry's murders.

Jay slowly slipped a toothpick out of his mouth. He sat calmly and listened while whittling on the toothpick.

Mario was surprised. "Where the hell did you get a toothpick?"

"Cops are so worried about checking pockets for weapons, needles, and whatever that they never look in your mouth."

"Do you know the damage one can do with a toothpick?" Mario shot back.

'No," Jay said. "Just a habit—I've chewed on a stick of some sort since I was a kid."

Mario asked a question that got Jay's attention. He was shocked to hear that Leon was the mayor's half-brother. His only response—life was unfair. Leon living on the very streets his brother, the mayor, promised he'd find places for the homeless to live.

"Politicians will promise anything to get elected," Mario said.

Howard, in his tender caring voice, asked questions. He'd prefer to grab Jay by the throat and raise him off the ground six inches. If he had information, he'd for sure give it up then.

"Two men are dead," Howard said. "Anything come to mind?"

Jay shouted that he knew nothing about their deaths. Howard pushed gently, asking about Leon and Barry's daily routines. Jay shook his head, then stopped. Howard immediately picked up on his emotions.

"What?" His nerves shattered when Howard stared him down.

Mario reached out. "If I find out you're holding back—I'll arrest you for obstruction."

Jay was fidgety and gulped down the rest of the Coke. He licked his lips, then said that Leon thought he was above all the other homeless people. Talking how he was a war hero and the government let him down. Other homeless individuals were just worthless people who didn't want to work and had no meaning in life.

"I didn't ask for this life," Jay shouted.

Howard encouraged him, Jay was fired up and might drop some useful info.

"Anything we might use," Howard said.

Jay hesitated, unsure of the importance, then explained a walk that Barry and he took with Leon. It was a Thursday about six months earlier. Leon passed Wallace Jackson in the street. It looked planned. One second, Leon was sitting on a bench, the next, he spotted Wallace and walked right up to him. They spoke for only seconds, and money was exchanged.

Mario encouraged him to continue, he did.

The three walked to a small hotel on Canal Street. Leon had received cash from the mayor to rent a room. Jay waited in the lobby. A half-hour later, Leon came down, showered, hair combed, looking a little less homeless. He was cleaned up enough to allow him in and out of the hotel lobby, which generally he'd be run out of quickly.

From the street, Jay watched Leon hand off a room keycard to the mayor. About two hours later, big-shot Leon took Jay and Barry up to the room and they showered. The three men used the place for the rest of the night and got to sleep in a bed on a real mattress for the first time in years.

The story was choppy. Howard slowed him down. "What was that all about?"

"I had the same question," Jay said. "About a week later, Leon showed me some pictures. He had them hiding behind a loose brick on a wall in an alley off Royal Street. Leon boasted how proud he was of taking them, his ace in the hole he called it. Thought they might fetch him more payoffs down the line if he showed them to the mayor."

As Leon explained to Jay, the mayor didn't want to be seen getting a room at the hotel, not under his name. Leon secured the place, with his military ID, still current, and the cash Wallace slipped him. When Leon gave Wallace a second keycard, he walked off and doubled back to the hotel through a side entrance. Then he took shelter near the room in the linen closet.

It wasn't too long after, Mayor Wallace showed up at the room alone. A few pictures were snapped from a cheap disposable camera. One picture caught the mayor and the room number. Shortly after, a well-dressed man showed up. He too was photographed with the room number exposed.

It was Leon's ticket out of the streets and the start of a new life. Mayor Wallace would pay thousands to keep the pictures out of the newspapers of him entering a hotel room and his lover following shortly afterwards.

"Any idea who the man was?" Mario asked.

Jay shook his head. "No, and Leon didn't recognize him either. But I can show you the pictures."

Howard stood ready. "We'll take my car."

Jay said there was no need. The pictures were in his backpack downstairs where he was processed into Central Lockup.

"You have pictures?" Mario snapped back.

"Well—Leon has no use for them."

Mario called for an officer to stand guard at the door while he and Howard went to check the pictures out.

At the processing cage, they waited for the officer on duty to bring the backpack from the evidence room. All personal items are kept in a locked room.

The green Army bag was placed on a table where Mario laid each item out. There it was, in a Walgreens photo packet. Six pictures of Wallace going into the room and a man in a suit followed minutes later. The time stamp put them going in eight minutes apart, staying thirty-five minutes, and departing separately.

Mario handed the pictures to Howard. "No doubt, it's Wallace. I don't know who this other guy is."

A questionable look came over Howard's face. His eyes beamed as if to penetrate the photo, then a blank stare.

"What? You know the guy?"

"I sat with him yesterday." Howard eyes fixed on the man's face. "It's Roberto Ferrari."

CHAPTER 24

JAY GATHERED HIS THINGS at the cage and processed out of jail, minus the pictures. Instructed not to leave town, in case Mario might want to ask more questions. He assured the police he could be found at his new job—Royal Street Grocery.

Mario and Howard arrived at the chief's office to well-wishes on their return to work. The police investigation had found the shooting justified. Most workers were happy for their clearance of any charges. Two cynical cops wished they'd never returned. Mario had no use for people who weren't team players. Their heads were fixed on climbing the ranks way too fast; he'd worked on a transfer for them that would soon be a reality.

A briefing with the chief brought them up to date. As expected, the mayor was on her ass to solve the bombing case. The two detectives held back their information on the sketchy information possibly involving the mayor. They had evidence, with Olivia's assistance. There would be only one attempt to take down a city official and their case better be rock solid.

They left the chief's office knowing their relationship

wasn't torched and she was behind them 100 percent. They had been through a lot. All three had skeletons in their closets and carried demands they had to live with.

The detectives arrived at the Eighth District station. On the way, Mario took a call from Emma Lou. Zack Nelson had been mugged and was in an emergency vehicle en route to Mercy Hospital.

Mario made a sharp turn over the trolley car tracks on Canal Street and flipped the blue light on the dashboard to flashing. With his siren blasting, he weaved in and out of traffic.

When they arrived at the hospital, Zack was in the emergency room being attended to by doctors. Two motorcycle police had escorted the emergency vehicle to the hospital and waited outside the ER for a statement. The detectives were allowed in the waiting area. Dave, Pearl Ann, and Emma Lou sat nervously with eyes focused on the ER doors, waiting for an update. All Emma Lou knew was that Zack had gone to the barbershop. She got a call from the barber that Zack was mugged on the block. A bus driver on the City Park route called the police.

"Was it a robbery?" Emma Lou looked at the detectives for answers.

Mario made a face and shrugged his shoulders. "We'll wait and see what Zack has to say."

Howard went out and talked to the two police officers. He learned there was an eyewitness. A woman jogging across the street in the park. She saw Zack hit the ground and a man jumped into a dark-colored sedan. The officer shared the last part of a Saints' license plate, A409. The woman was positive on the numbers.

Howard called the plate to dispatch and within minutes got the name and address of the owner. Howard went back to the waiting room to find Mario and Emma Lou in with Zack. He was told he'd be allowed in when one of them came out. He flashed his badge and was allowed in immediately.

Zack sat up in the bed, a bad gash on his head from when he hit the ground. Emma Lou was asked to leave, and Mario drilled him with questions.

Zack raised his hand. "Hold up, Mario. Never seen the guys before but could pick one or both out of a lineup. The kid, Logan, sent them; he wants his two hundred grand."

Mario's head was about to explode. The investigation into the mayor had slowed him from making the case on Logan's computer scam.

"This punk thinks he can go gangster on Zack? I'll break him in two." Howard slipped through the information he got from the officer. It was time for them to make an arrest on these thugs and put a case together against Logan. Zack was warned not to discuss Logan's involvement with him to anyone. Not even his trusted friends.

The detectives were fired up and headed to the owner of the car's address on Coliseum Street in the Garden District. They stopped and parked the car a few houses away and went on foot to the front door.

"Upscale neighborhood," Howard said. "Not the kind of house you'll find a thug living."

Mario gave three hard knocks at the door "Well, we're about to find out."

The door opened slowly and a woman peeked out, asking if she could help them. Mario flashed his badge and announced they were police.

"We're looking for Gerald Miller." Howard towered over the woman and got a look into the house. A door slammed at the side entrance. Howard spotted a man running down the alley to the rear of the house. "Runner!" He jumped over the porch rail and chased the man. At the back of the yard, a man fell to the ground after a failed attempt to scale a brick wall. A second try was interrupted by the clicking sound of Howard's gun when the hammer locked in place.

"Bet I can blow your leg off before your next try." Howard reached with one hand and pulled the guy up.

In the kitchen, Mario secured the wife, and Howard brought the man in with cuffs on. Plopped him into a chair and asked what he was running from.

The woman spoke up, defending and explaining he worked for her and lived in the cottage at the rear of the vast grounds. He was a housekeeper for everything exterior, gardening, windows, painting, you name it, Akbar did the job.

Akbar spoke broken English. Said he ran when he heard "police." In his country, police meant one thing, jail for a few weeks, then death. The woman identified herself as Becky Miller. Akbar was from Africa living with her and her husband. He was a student at Tulane University.

Mario peeked at his notes again. "I'm looking for Gerald Miller."

"He's not available."

Howard rocked on his heels, the woman visibly uncomfortable. "Make him available."

Mario calculated the circumstances. The woman, well-dressed, educated, the property on the high side of upscale. Over the woman's shoulder, he saw expensive, antique pieces in the living room. Add the exchange student, and it didn't fit the profile of a thug or criminal.

The woman recommended they visit her husband, Dr. Gerald Miller, at work in an hour when he'd finished a lecture at Tulane.

Mario apologized. They must have had the wrong address.

Mrs. Miller, a pleasant woman under the problematic circumstances, asked the detectives for help. Someone had broken into her car, and she wondered what division of the police department she should call. Her insurance company said a police report was required.

She was shopping at the mall and when she returned to the parking lot, her car was in a different parking space. The driver's window was broken and wires from under the dashboard pulled out.

"Crazy," she said. "A laptop worth fifteen hundred, clothes she'd purchased earlier at Macy's in the back seat. All left behind."

Mario and Howard gave a side glance at each other and almost simultaneously asked to see the car. When the overhead garage door opened, Mario spotted the Saints' license plate ending in A409.

Mario explained the car might have been used in a crime and called for a patrol car. Then he called Olivia and asked for a rush on forensics. He was hoping for a useful fingerprint from the car's steering wheel. Olivia came to the house herself. She processed the steering wheel, dashboard, radio dials, and got a sizeable solid thumbprint on the air conditioner knob.

The crime involving Zack was personal and no doubt prompted by Logan Taylor. Mario needed a lead on who Logan hired for the job. The detectives followed Olivia back to her office. She had a name and a work address within minutes. They stood by the printer, waiting for a picture of Bowie David. If he didn't attack Zack, he'd have a lot of explaining about what he was doing in Becky Miller's car. Armed with the information, the detectives headed to the hospital. With a phone call to the ER to see if Zack had been moved to a room, they learned he'd been released.

Riverside Inn was a mile away. They found Zack and friends in the dining hall with afternoon coffee and cinnamon rolls the kitchen made every evening.

One glimpse at the pictures and Zack identified the guy. "That's the asshole."

Before they rushed out, they were offered coffee and a roll but declined, instead taking one each in a napkin for the road. Neither could refuse sweets, especially the cinnamon rolls they were introduced to on the first day they walked into the Riverside Inn dining room.

The work address Olivia found was from a bartender's liquor permit needed to serve drinks. The car pulled curbside of a bar too familiar on Bourbon Street. They both agreed it was a bar owned by Lorenzo Savino at one time. Who owned it now or if it was tied up in litigation after Lorenzo's death, they weren't sure.

Mario moved his unmarked police car a few bars down. They put their coats in the trunk and pulled their shirts over their guns attached to their belts. With their neckties off and shirts opened, they strolled in and bellied up to the bar. As expected mid-afternoon, the place was empty.

They ordered two beers from a bartender. She returned with the beers in one hand and a dirty rag in the other. Smeared the bar with the cloth, dropped two napkins, and placed the beers on top. "Shift change—I'll leave the bill. My coworker, Bowie, will be out in a second."

"No problem." Mario threw a twenty on the bill. "Keep the change."

She smiled, then scooped up the bill and the cash. "Thanks."

A man came from the storage room carrying four bottles of whiskey and replaced empties on the mirrored shelf.

Mario got a glimpse of the big guy's name tag and nudged Howard. "That's our man."

"Twice Zack's size." Howard mumbled. "I'd like a one-on-one with him."

"Y'all need anything?" Bowie asked.

Mario played tourist, asking places to eat and the best place for nightlife. Bowie laughed, said no one ever asked him where the action was when having a drink on Bourbon Street.

"My friend, if you can't find a place to have fun in the French Quarter, you're not looking too hard."

"Bowie. Don't see that name too often." Mario got him talking. "Is that after the guy with the knife? Jim Bowie?"

"No, sorry to say my mother was a David Bowie fan in the seventies. My last name is David. So she thought Bowie David would be a fun name."

Mario and Howard got Bowie talking, they ordered another round and tipped a twenty. They put on a good act as farmers from Talladega, Alabama, who didn't get to the big city too often. It was Bowie who brought up ladies, and Mario snapped up the suggestion. Nothing had changed, even with Lorenzo Savino dead. The bar still hustled. Ladies flowing freely throughout the ground floor keeping everyone drinking. When an opportunity of a sucker comes along, he's invited upstairs where it gets costly.

Bowie gave a nod to a coworker, and he took over the bar while Bowie walked Mario and Howard to the stairs.

"Can five hundred get me some fun?" Mario asked.

Bowie grinned. "You'll be happy with the results."

At the top of the stairs, a guy stood. No one was getting any farther without an escort from the bartender. A piss-poor screening process, Mario thought when passing the thug.

They were taken to a room. Four women sat at another bar, called the VIP room, where customers picked the gal of their dreams.

Mario whispered in Bowie's ear, said it was a little embarrassing and could they talk privately. They were taken to an empty bedroom. Bowie looked out a window down at Bourbon Street. Howard guarded the door.

"Let me guess." Bowie smiled. "You're uncomfortable—not looking for a woman. You think you're the first gay man who walked through our doors?"

"You got my number," Mario said.

Bowie pointed out another bar down the street that could cater to his needs.

Mario cut him short. "The only need I have is for you to tell me who hired you to rough up Zack Nelson."

Bowie's eyes scanned the room. He was big but wasn't sure he could take both of them. He shouted for security, and within seconds, the thug at the end of the hall rushed in. Howard closed and locked the door behind him.

With one swift kick, Howard took out the guy's right knee. Backhanded, he hit him on the left side of his face. Off balance to the right, a robust left blow to the rib cage put him curled up on the floor.

"I know Logan hired you." Mario backed Bowie into a corner. "Just admit it."

"Don't know what you're talking about."

"Give me the right answer or you'll be eating through a straw for the next few weeks." Mario was pressing him against the wall by his neck. "Who?" More pressure was applied. Bowie pulled the best he could, but Mario locked his elbows into his chest.

"Logan," Bowie said in a whisper. "Wanted me to shake him up."

Mario pulled his hands away. In poor judgment, Bowie took a swing at Mario. He missed, Mario didn't. Three solid hits, one to the face, the stomach, and the back of the head, sent Bowie down to the floor.

"This one is for Zack," he said and added a swift kick to the ribs.

Mario called dispatch. Minutes later, cops cleared the floor of the ladies and arrested Bowie. Paramedics saw to the other guy, who hadn't moved since Howard laid into him.

Mario could have gone to Bee's Computer Shop and quickly arrested Logan, but that would have been too easy on him. Howard stayed in the car. Mario took a deep breath and gathered his thoughts before entering.

"Hi," he told the woman at the front counter. A flash of his badge got him access to the back room where Logan was alone, bent over a computer.

"I don't want trouble." Mario strolled in, giving computer boy false confidence. He jumped at the opportunity.

"Give me my damn money." His eyes lit like fire. "Give me Zack's password and all will be fine."

"I'll take you to Zack. He'll return your money. Just don't hurt him again."

"Yeah, man," Logan said. "I just want my money, or next time it won't be just a bump on his head."

With the car's tinted windows, Logan didn't see Howard in the back seat. It was too late once they pulled off.

"Who's he?"

"Just a friend." Mario continued the act. "Zack is waiting, he wants this over."

"Yeah," Logan said, "We'll call it a misunderstanding."

"Call it what you will." Mario turned the car into Big Gabe's Car Wash.

"What the hell, you're getting your car washed?" Logan was pulled from the car by both arms and carried to the house at the rear of the car wash.

Big Gabe leaned against the fence and gave a nod of his head as he held the gate open. In the shotgun house, Logan sat at the kitchen table. Ten minutes earlier, he was an arrogant shit who'd pulled off some cybercrimes that netted him six figures quickly. No telling how much money he'd continue to take from defenseless people, if he hadn't ripped off a cop.

"Scared?" Mario asked. "Because you should be."

Mario roamed the floor like a preacher on a Sunday morning. He rattled on about legal justice for what Logan had done. Return of some money, a reasonable attorney, he'd walk. Still enough cash left to live on for the next ten years.

Logan tried to speak. Mario held his hand up, cut him off, and continued walking almost in a circle. Howard stood in the corner with a grin. It made Logan more nervous than Mario's unpredictable waltzing around.

"Gangs prefer street justice over a court of law. Guilty, a gang would take you out, usually within twenty-four hours. In court, you might get off, short sentence, or get out early, because you're so good in prison. Street justice wants an eye for an eye."

Mario sat across from Logan at the table. "Taking an old man's money, then ordering an attack on him, makes my friend, Zack, nervous."

"He took all my money," Logan shouted. "A hell of a lot more than I took from him."

"True." Mario smiled, not the least interested. "You got physical. Zack Nelson will live in fear every time he walks to a barbershop or a drugstore. Sitting alone on a park bench, he'll always ask—am I safe?"

Logan wasn't a small guy, but no match for two cops. He eyeballed the screen door a few times and was at the right angle to make a dash. One thing he knew for sure, he was twenty years younger and a hell of a lot faster on foot.

Mario leaned against the stove, putting him and Howard farther away from the exit. Logan peeked at the unlocked screen door again. Mario picked up on it the first time. He gave Logan all the opportunity needed to make a run.

Mario pounded the table. His fist rattled the loose legs. "I've had enough of talk. I think it's time to kick some ass."

Before Mario got all the words out, Logan hit the screen door with both arms. The door hinges broke, and Logan was gone. Within seconds, he was thrown headfirst back into the house. He ran into a six-foot, eight-inch tree trunk—Big Gabe. "Where the hell are you going?"

Mario picked Logan up from the floor and landed a punch straight into his stomach. This time Big Gabe stepped aside and Logan hit the ground face down, gasping for breath. "It's not quite street justice, but it'll have to do."

Howard cuffed Logan. "You're under arrest, asshole."

CHAPTER 25

An attorney for Logan Taylor stood in front of a judge and said the money transfers were a misunderstanding between Logan and his clients. The real crime was the beating Logan took during the arrest. He demanded justice and for his client to be released.

Howard watched from the back of the courtroom. The DA's office had its top attorney on the case. The entire hearing didn't last fifteen minutes.

Mario raised his head from a pile of paperwork scattered across his desk, "Was Pamela on her game?"

"Absolutely," Howard said, taking a seat.

The district attorney's office was represented by Pamela Jones, an up-and-coming attorney. With a few years under her belt, graduating with top honors from Loyola University, she quickly became Mario's favorite prosecuting attorney. Not because he was an alumnus of Loyola, so he tried to make people believe.

Pamela had interviewed the two police officers, Mario and Howard, separately and came away with the same understanding. If Logan hadn't resisted arrest and run, he wouldn't have run smack into a tree. Any cuts and bruises were from his own stupidity, an unsuccessful escape.

A judge of thirty years on the bench agreed the issues were wire fraud, computer hacking, and outright taking advantage of people for monetary gain. Adding the assault on Zack Nelson would put Logan behind bars for a long time.

Logan said he would give up all the money to save his ass. The judge didn't fall for his generosity. Howard chuckled. "Still could get five to eight years."

Mario looked back at the folder in front of him. "Creep deserves every minute."

Mario thumbed through Olivia's final report in Leon and Barry's file. They both had a bullet to the forehead. His question was how did two people get shot, six feet apart? Were there two shooters?

In Leon's folder were crime scene photos. There was also a picture of a metal tray at the morgue showing the possessions found in his pockets. A cell phone, some change, three one-dollar bills, and a dirty handkerchief. The phone, a throwaway, had sixty minutes left, and the only calls made were to the same number, four times, since purchased two days ago.

Mario checked with Olivia and found that the calls were traced to another disposable phone. Her crew found where the phone was purchased and looked at the video footage showing everyone in and out of the convenience store in the last three days.

Olivia had Mario and Howard come down to her office to view the film. She'd reviewed the tape twice and recognized no one who bought one of the six phones over the last three days. One person the face recognition program picked up had a felony charge. Further checking showed the man had served his time for tax evasion and was released from prison a year earlier. He was flagged but not considered a suspect, due to the violent nature of the current crime they were investigating.

Mario picked up lunch, and he and Howard headed to the police forensic building on Broad. Olivia ate a quarter of an Italian muffuletta and swore she had gained ten pounds hanging with these two detectives.

"Do you guy eat—salads, once in a while?"

Mario pointed out the carrots, onions, and olives on the sandwich.

"Yeah!" Olivia shot back. "Olive salad, drenched in olive oil, salami, provolone, and who knows what else?"

Mario grinned. "But, it's good."

"Damn you, Mario," she said and took the last bite of the sandwich.

During lunch, her assistant had edited the film. A short tape was made of only the six people of interest. Olivia and the two detectives gathered over a computer screen while the assistant flipped through the screenshots. The third one was the man Olivia said was ruled out. Howard asked to zoom in on the fourth picture, the guy had a hat on—Howard noticed something. "I could swear that guy is Kory Barnes. Look at the nose, chin, lips."

"The mayor's assistant?" Olivia asked. A nod of heads between Mario and Howard confirmed her question.

Olivia gave a confused grin. "How would Leon know

Kory? They come from two different parts of the world. One with political ambitions and the other is—"

"Their world is connected," Mario said. "Kory works for Wallace, and Leon is Wallace's half-brother. My guess is if it's him, he bought the phone for the mayor."

It took a while for Olivia to be brought up to speed on the case. With another piece to the puzzle confirmed, Leon had talked to whoever had the phone purchased from the convenience store. Number one suspect was Wallace; number two Kory. The question was why.

Mario carried Leon's folder with him and spread the contents on a desk. He had a question about the toothpick that had been found. Olivia pulled a stack of snapshots taken at the scene. Halfway through the pile, a photograph of Leon surfaced. A different angle showed a toothpick near his hair on the grass.

"Son of a bitch, Olivia," Mario shouted. A reaction he regretted, then he spoke at a whisper. "Did you think this might be important to tell me?"

"Yes, detective, that's why it's on the third page of my report." She pointed. "You read my report like you look through girly magazines." Olivia hated when Mario flew off the handle. He was usually wrong, and this time was no different. She hurried to the coffee room; he followed.

"And what does that mean?"

She jumped in his face. "Means just like your girly magazines, you went straight to the pictures. Not once reading what supported the photos."

Howard laughed. "She's got you there, brother. You always go to the centerfold first."

Mario flipped through two pages of small print. A number described each picture. On the third page, which Mario hadn't gotten around to reading, the text described the toothpick. It was inconclusive. The wood was too small for a fingerprint to be lifted. Saliva in the hair failed to match anyone in the police database.

Mario's head lifted, his face beet red, embarrassed, he pointed at the last line on the description. It read that the depth of the spit embedded into Leon's hair was forcefully driven.

"That was taken from the coroner's report," Olivia said.

Mario and Howard's eyes locked; they both came to the same conclusion. Mario said it first. "This is personal, the killer knew Leon and had a vendetta."

Howard added, "To kill someone and then spit on the body—that's the final 'screw you.'"

Mario turned his attitude down and apologized twice for jumping on Olivia. Said he'd make it up with dinner that night. She rolled her eyes.

"You Italians. Everything is built around food."

Mario went into a stare, his eyes glazed. "Oh, my god!"

The report stated the saliva failed to match anyone in the police database. Mario suggested that Olivia ask her friend at military intelligence for another favor.

CHAPTER 26

GLENN MACY FIRST MET Mario DeLuca at Loyola University. They were never friends in school, only had one journalism class mutually, and gave a casual nod when seated near each other at a lecture. After college, Mario went on to the police academy and worked his way through the ranks quickly. Glenn took the first job offered from the Times-Picayune newspaper as a reporter.

Twenty years passed before their paths crossed again. Mario's name bugged Glenn until he hunted down an old dusty graduation photo album and found Mario's picture. It wasn't until a year ago that circumstances brought them together. Mario kept Glenn out of a report that would have revealed he and Roxy Blum were lovers—a situation Glenn had been working up the courage to tell his wife of fifteen years. Roxy testified in a case that allowed Mario to close it and get national media attention for solving a twenty-year-old bank robbery.

Since then, they'd stayed close, had lunches, and Mario took Olivia on a date to Roxy's nightclub. He was a talented, gay man, lead singer in a transvestite group. Many people said he was much prettier as a woman than as a man.

Mario knocked lightly on the front door of Roxy's Esplanade Avenue home. At eight in the morning, Roxy would be asleep and Glenn probably getting ready for work. He was right. Glenn opened the door in a whisper and met Mario on the porch.

He had been on the receiving end of many exclusives stories from Mario, and to date everyone proved 100 percent accurate. The exclusives gained his newspaper, the Big Easy Voice, publicity, and subscriptions had doubled over the last year. Big city media outlets published the same article days later—old news didn't sell newspapers.

A press conference at city hall in two hours would prove Mario's tip. He gave Glenn another exclusive story that other news outlets would envy. This tip would set off an explosion like a bomb. Mario detailed the story and suggested Glenn have newspapers ready for distribution. Glenn's eyes showed worriment, but he trusted his source and didn't hesitate to agree.

Mario had another stop before the press conference and would need every bit of an hour before heading to city hall. He arrived at Dumaine Street, then parked like every other time in a no parking zone in front of Riverside Inn. Howard and Zack sat at a table alone. His friends understood it was official police business. Mario and Howard had hashed the situation over so much, they questioned if they were overreacting. Bringing in a third opinion from a veteran detective like Zack might help.

Over coffee, they confidentially explained the mayor's assistance in buying a prepaid cell phone, the toothpick near Leon's hair, and Roberto Ferrari wanting Mario dead.

The seventy-two-year-old retired detective still had a sharp mind. Sometimes, former cops can look at a case differently and bring positive results. They could tell when Zack was on his A game. His eyes went side to side, like wheels in his brain moved them while combing through the facts. He questioned Kory Barnes's background, and Howard assured him that Kory was squeaky clean, not even a speeding ticket.

Zack focused on Jay, the only living homeless guy of the three. Pushing hard might get him talking. He knew where the photos had been kept and why Leon held on to them. Jay could have jumped the gun, tried to blackmail Leon or the mayor. To hit the mayor up for the money, he had to have Leon out the way. Barry might have been in the way and caught a bullet too. When Zack got on a roll, the words spewed.

As for Roberto, Zack's feelings aligned with the detectives. If a mob boss wants someone dead, they'd better get a running start and not stop until they got to some undeveloped country. Even then, it would only be a matter of time before they were found and killed.

Howard laid out a plan he'd thought about ever since he returned from New Jersey. With Michael dead, there were no family members to retaliate if Roberto was killed. Next in line was Bobby G. Most would think that if something happened to Roberto, it would be Bobby's doing to become the new boss of bosses. Either way, Mario would be long forgotten and the person hired for the hit would take the money and run and not finish the job.

This wag-the-dog approach had been used by many.

Some said wars were begun to get the heat off the heads of governments. Too much lousy publicity about an official, and the government invaded some country. Then the next morning, the news was full of war history and why the United States had to take down some poor, defenseless country. If Roberto were dead, Bobby would have too much on his plate within his own organization to worry about Mario.

Zack knocked off the cobwebs from one of his old stories and talked about his run-in with a criminal. A well-connected guy wanted Zack, a detective close to charging him with murder, out of his life and would do whatever it took. One failed attempt prompted Zack not to wait for the second try. On Wednesday nights, Zack knew that the guy ate alone at his favorite restaurant. Zack followed him to a dimly lit parking lot. When the guy went into the restaurant, Zack parked next to his car and waited. When the thug returned, Zack stood between the two vehicles and surprised him. It didn't take much to provoke the guy to the point he reached for his gun. Zack already had a stun gun in his hand and zapped him to the ground. With gloves, Zack slipped on a thin, plastic poncho and pulled the thug's gun from his coat. The man, barely awake, saw his own pistol pointed at his chin; then Zack discharged the weapon. With the body limp, his finger was placed on the trigger.

The thug was still alive when Zack walked to a dumpster and placed the gloves and the poncho in a box and set it on fire. Checking the criminal, he was hardly breathing, but alive. Zack waited until he took his last breath, then called

911, identified himself as Detective Zack Nelson, and told them to send police and a firetruck.

Mario and Howard were stunned that the man they'd known for a few years had dropped an incredible story on them.

"Were you charged with anything?" Mario asked.

"The evidence backed my story. A second attempt to kill me resulted in the man pulling his gun recklessly and he 'accidentally' shot himself. I did my part and called nine one one, once I was sure he was dead."

Zack showed no remorse, even thirty years later. There was nothing the police could do to protect him. It would have ended with one of them dead. Zack chose to live.

"Street justice was around long before I was a cop," Zack said. "Now and then, it's justified."

A waiter placed a fresh carafe of coffee on the table. They were all ready for another round of caffeine.

The table went silent for a minute. Zack looked exhausted from reliving his past. Mario's thoughts bounced around his head like a metallic ball in a pinball machine.

Mario looked at his watch, he had thirty minutes to get to the mayor's press conference. He thanked Zack for hearing them out and walked away with a plan. Risky, but if it worked, it would be enough to seal an indictment against the mayor.

Howard pulled Mario's arm. "Cover for me? Two days at most. Zack gave me an idea."

When questioned where he was going, Howard gave a smile. When Mario pushed and mentioned New Jersey, his smile broadened.

CHAPTER 27

THE CONFERENCE ROOM AT city hall was packed with TV cameras and reporters sitting up front. Glenn sat four rows back, giving him a view of the cameras and everyone in the room. Present, supporting the mayor, were some church people, including Pastor Ignatius Green, the man some say got the mayor elected, and his inner circle of political advisers. Then there was the chief of police, district attorney, and heads of other departments who opposed him—but never openly.

Mario took a seat in the back, just as Kory Barnes walked to the microphone. The room went silent anticipating the start. He went over the rules of the press conference to keep questions to the subject of the mayor's announcement. It was the same crap he said each time, but the meeting always got out of hand.

The mayor was introduced by Kory "the weasel," a nickname Mario gave him just that morning.

Applause sounded. Some clapped wholeheartedly; others made little effort. The opening statement was predictable: how in shambles the city was before he took office. It got him another round of applause by half the room. It took fifteen minutes for him to get to an announcement everyone knew was coming. His official declaration of re-election and promise to clean up the city of its deplorable streets, neighborhoods, and the influx of crime.

Mario overheard one reporter say, "Didn't he promise the same three years ago when he was elected?"

When questions bombarded the mayor, he handled each one with a cool head and a smile. For years, the political machine had allowed the city to decline, and one person couldn't fix it in one term. He rambled about all the things he would do before the year was out and how much more he could do by being re-elected.

The speech made Mario think of Truman, his recently departed friend. Truman hated Mayor Wallace Jackson; they had gone to the same high school. He declared Wallace a shyster from early on, and the mayor did nothing to improve his image for Truman till the day he died.

The mayor answered eight or nine questions and handled them well, or maybe he was just a good liar, which Mario favored.

It was showtime when Glenn raised his hand, and Mario could only hope this would go as planned.

"Glenn," the mayor said, pointing at him.

He stood. "Thank you, sir. If elected, will you be looking outside of Louisiana for a new police chief?"

Glenn had picked on something close to the mayor's heart. He wanted a replacement since the day he took office. The present chief of police made it easy for the mayor, when he'd announced two months earlier he'd retire at the end of the mayor's term.

"Good question," the mayor said, with a broad grin. "I have my eye on two people, both with years of experience. One from Los Angeles and the other from Baltimore."

Glenn's follow-up question was how would the city come up with the money to attract such high-profile candidates? The mayor's answer redirected the issue to the city council members. The ball was in their court to step up with the salary demanded by quality law enforcement candidates, or the city would continue to decline and the criminals would take control.

The questions were put together correctly, and Mario sat waiting for the punch to the gut that hopefully would get the reaction he wanted.

"Thank you all for coming," Wallace said, with a big wave.

Glenn shouted above the clapping, "Mr. Mayor! Please, one last question."

Wallace's frown showed he was annoyed. "Make it quick."

"Can you comment on the two men found dead in Lafayette Square?"

"I haven't been briefed, so I can't comment." His body went stiff as a board, eyes glassy with anger—a nerve was hit.

Then Glenn came with the final blow and shouted, "Sir! They were homeless men. One was Leon Mason, an Army veteran and your brother."

If the mayor was like anyone else in the room, he couldn't think over the uproar of follow-up questions. Wallace left the room in front of an entourage of staff.

Glenn held a newspaper over his head, displaying the headline of the Big Easy Voice: "Mayor Wallace Jackson's Half-Brother Murdered" with a subtitle below, "Why Are Army Veterans Living On The Streets?"

Mario scanned the chaos of reporters converging on Glenn, wanting more of the story. He gave them the perfect reply. "The Big Easy Voice is on sale at newsstands."

Head nods between Glenn and Mario were exchanged. Another exclusive for Glenn and an outlet for Mario to get information out without involvement, it was a win-win for both.

At the Eighth District station, Mario checked in with his number-two man, Drexel Lawson. He wasn't officially named yet but was the most qualified and next to become a lieutenant. Few could replace Truman in Mario's mind, but he had to decide on his number-two man soon, or the chief would choose for him.

Checking his messages, he found one from Ralph Givens and returned the call. Mario had lunch planned with the chief in an hour, so he met Ralph at the steps of One Shell Square.

Getting out the police cruiser, parked in a freight zone, Mario spotted Ralph coming down the steps of the building to the street level. Ralph owed Mario his new life as an investment banker. He could have spent years in jail, but with Mario's help, he slipped past criminal charges Now he was making serious money in what he did best, investing. He swore this would be the last time he'd do anything unlawful. Mario laughed, as it was the third time Ralph had made such a statement. Mario knew Ralph could never turn down a request. The criminal element intrigued him—he couldn't resist.

"What do you have?" Mario asked.

"That woman, Julie Wong, came through for us." He looked around and slipped Mario a piece of paper as if someone was watching.

Ralph had tried for days to hack Wallace Jackson's email account. His city hall account was a piece of cake, but there were no conversations between him and Roberto, as expected. Wallace's personal email was an issue, so he tried a back-door approach, helped by Julie.

Julie provided all the information needed to take a shot at Roberto's computer. If they could get a few emails, along with the pictures of Wallace and Roberto meeting in a hotel room, that should be enough for a DA investigation—enough info to get started.

"I did all I could," Ralph said. "Broke every cyberlaw there is and still came up short."

"Can it be done?" Mario waited for an honest reply.

"Technology is manmade. Any computer can be hacked. Just need to find the right person."

Mario's watch alarm sounded; it was time to meet the chief. Ralph would keep trying to get through Roberto's firewall, and Mario would attempt to get some help. Olivia knew a few people with computer skills, but she wasn't sure they could be trusted or would be willing to risk their careers to take down a politician.

The chief sat at a table for two at a deli on Conti Street. Mario wanted to meet but not at her office. If seen in the deli by fellow officers, it would look like a casual lunch and not official business. A hostess walked Mario to the table; he sat.

"It has to be important," she said, "for you to buy lunch."

"Maybe I want a huge favor?"

"Then we better head over to Antoine's Restaurant," she said with a smile.

They ordered red beans and rice, Creole style, the special of the day. Mario talked about a case while waiting for lunch. When the food arrived, he changed subjects. The chief was the only person he could trust. He opened with saying that the mayor was dirty. She laughed, it was common knowledge; it just couldn't be proven. Mario added—until now.

The pictures of Wallace and Roberto were carefully shown. Her first reaction was much like Mario's, Wallace had a gay lover. Maybe twenty years ago, being gay would have gotten a mayor to resign, but not today. Mario pointed at Roberto and refreshed her memory of the well-dressed man from the East Coast. Her first reaction was much like everyone who saw the pictures. Why was the mayor of New Orleans meeting secretly in a hotel with a mafia boss?

Mario got to the point, asking for her support if he came up with proof that Wallace was involved with the death of Leon and was pushing the gambling agenda so his newfound business partner could come into the city and take over the food, liquor, and beer distributions.

The chief pulled off the heel of the French bread that came with the lunch and gracefully dropped it on her plate.

"It's the only way to finish off a dish this good," she

said. Then she pushed the bread around the plate, picking up the juice of the red beans remaining.

Mario agreed and did the same. "It's the way I was raised."

Chief Parks took her time replying, dabbed her lips with the cloth napkin, then pulled out a compact and touched up her lipstick. "You're asking for me to make a career decision?"

"With solid proof, it's a career builder to the next level." Mario waited for a reply.

It took a few more seconds for a response. "Get me the proof, and I'll walk it to the attorney general myself. Has to be rock solid."

"Absolutely, madam chief."

CHAPTER 28

A GULFSTREAM JET DESCENDED and landed at the Atlantic City airport. It wasn't uncommon to see private jets shuttling casino high rollers in and out of the city every day. This jet had a well-paid ground crew and one person in the tower who adjusted paperwork for Julie Wong's plane as nothing more than a fuel stop. The worker topped off the fuel and got back in his truck only to find a passenger, Howard Blitz, sitting next to him. He was paid well to look the other way, not ask questions, and drop him inside the building away from cameras.

Julie flew to New York for shopping. If she didn't hear from Howard in three hours, she'd fly back to New Orleans, and assume Howard was dead.

A town car waited at the curb, motor running and air-conditioning on high. Howard took to the back seat, the dark-tinted glass kept him out of view.

Julie wanted no part of Howard's undertaking but provided surveillance of Bobby G. She was right on target. It was Wednesday afternoon and Bobby G. was at his most frequented hotel and casino between noon and four, holed up in a suite with his girlfriend.

A hundred-dollar bill to Tony, the bell captain, got him a keycard for entry to any room. Howard was only interested in one suite, 2710, overlooking the ocean.

It had been Bobby's Wednesday comp room for months. He wasn't the smartest; he'd never changed his driving route to the casino, the suite, or the woman and her pick-up point. He could have easily been picked off, if he was the target. Bobby was an egotistical asshole and followed the mafia tradition perfectly. On date night, he'd parade his wife through the casino a few times before entering the restaurant. Dressed in an outfit from Fifth Avenue that cost more than most of the blackjack dealers made in a week. His wife on the weekends, and a midweek walkthrough with a flashy bimbo. Why? To show he was rich, a ladies' man, and could do whatever he wanted. He was the right-hand man to the most powerful mob boss, Roberto Ferrari. He didn't need a bodyguard. Any man who attempted to harm Bobby could expect an army of Roberto's people hunting him down. His death would not be quick or painless, and he'd beg for a bullet to the head.

What Bobby was about to learn was that Howard Blitz was not any man, and he always got what he went after. To an assassin, a person's status didn't matter who they were or how rich. Nothing mattered. If someone was on Howard's radar, he would accomplish his objective.

The room keycard slipped into the electric door reader. One click, and Howard was in the living room. The usual gaudy decorating for a casino suite didn't disappoint; it matched anything in Las Vegas, except for a view of a beautiful ocean and not piles of sand dunes. In that respect, Atlantic City was one step ahead of Las Vegas.

Howard pulled his gun, the silencer attached, ready to take out Bobby if need be and the woman would have to go too. He heard talking but couldn't tell if it came from the bedroom or the bathroom. Water splashed, then the sound of a motor pushing air bubbles at high speed confirmed they were isolated in the bathroom.

Howard rounded the corner of the bedroom, picked up Bobby's gun from the nightstand, tucked it in his belt, then slipped along the wall until he saw their reflections in the mirror. Bobby, preoccupied, had his head buried in his bimbo's breasts. He put his champagne glass to the side to engage with two hands. He surfaced from her well-rounded chest to the barrel of a gun between his eyes.

"Get out," Howard motioned to the woman. She jumped at the opportunity, gathered her clothes, and left, barely dressed.

Bobby reached for a towel and walked at gunpoint to a chair in the bedroom. "You're making a big mistake." He got a good look at Howard. "You're the guy who met with Roberto last week."

"Good memory—now shut up and listen."

He said that Roberto had hired Howard to kill Bobby. He tried to convince Bobby, but he wasn't buying. Then he pushed more lies that he hoped were believable.

"Roberto is certain you killed his nephew, Michael," Howard said, and waited for his denial.

"You're crazy. Why would I do that?"

"Well, according to Roberto, you were in New Orleans

the day before Michael was killed." This was the part of Julie's information that had to be faultless. "Maybe you stayed an extra day? Did you?" There was no reply. Julie was correct again.

With Michael out of the way, Bobby would be next in line for the boss. Howard took a seat on the bed across from him. The gun never left its fixed aim at Bobby's head.

"Roberto firmly believes with Michael out of the way, you'll make a run at him."

Howard let the news sink in and saw Bobby was giving it some consideration.

"Bullshit. Michael would never be boss. He was weak and hated by the entire crew."

"Family is family, doesn't matter if the crew likes or dislikes him," Howard said, stone-faced, never blinking. "Michael was next in line."

Bobby made a desperate move. "Whatever Roberto is paying, I'll double."

Howard laughed; it didn't work that way. A hit man never double-crossed his client. It's not suitable for referrals.

Bobby took another shot. "How much, fifty? I'll pay a hundred grand."

Howard sat, giving a creepy grin, imagining putting a bullet in Bobby's head. "Keep your money. I need Mario DeLuca alive and Roberto—let's say—gone."

It opened dialog and Bobby jumped at the opportunity. Howard negotiating Bobby's life for Roberto's. He didn't care how it was done, but Roberto had to disappear forever. Then Bobby would be the new boss. Howard saw his idea was being considered. Bobby was ready to agree to anything to get out of this jam. Howard reinforced that if Roberto wasn't permanently out of the picture, he'd hunt Bobby down and it wouldn't be a pleasant death.

Bobby said that there was a meeting between Roberto and Bobby planned for the next day. The only other person with them would be Sal, the bodyguard. Bobby guaranteed that Roberto would disappear; he'd become the new boss and all contracts on Mario would be canceled. Howard wondered about Sal having a vital role in flipping against Roberto. Bobby unquestionably believed Sal was the right man for the job.

Howard lowered his gun and placed it in his holster. Then reviewed what would happen if Bobby wavered. Just like Howard got the drop on Bobby in the hotel room, he'd hunt him down until he suffered a horrible death. First, he'd learn his daughter and her nanny died in a car accident on the way to school one day. Then, he'd come home to his murdered wife sitting at the kitchen table. Howard would then assure Bobby it could all have been avoided if he'd only have followed through with his promise of taking out Roberto.

"Are you in?" Howard asked.

"I promise," Bobby said, to the point of pleading.

"Two days." He emptied the bullets from Bobby's gun and threw them at his feet. Then dropping the weapon at the door, he walked out.

From the Atlantic City airport, Howard hopped a helicopter to LaGuardia Airport and joined Julie for the flight back to New Orleans.

"It's good to see you alive," Julie said, as the jet taxied to the runway.

"No doubt on my part." Howard smiled, as he was thrust deep into the seat when the jet lifted off the ground. "There were only two possible results of my meeting Bobby. Me dead today or Roberto dead within two days."

CHAPTER 29

THE EIGHTH DISTRICT STATION had the worst parking, even for cops. The police commissioner wanted easy access for police in the heart of the French Quarter, so a station sat on narrow Royal Street with no consideration of parking. Olivia did what all cops did—parked half on the street with two wheels on the sidewalk. Something locals and tourists received a ticket for and a two-hundred-dollar fee for towing the vehicle.

Olivia strolled into Mario's office unannounced and closed the door behind her.

"It's never a good sign when you come to my side of town before noon." He lifted his head from the mound of paperwork on his desk.

She hit him with the lousy news before taking a seat. The saliva in Leon's hair was inconclusive.

It was something Mario was sure would tie Jay to the murder. He rocked back and forth in his desk chair. The toothpick was Jay's signature look, he'd said it himself. Mario pictured Jay leaning over Leon and spitting after he shot him. It was the perfect solution. "Inconclusive?" Mario said, chewing on his lip, staring into space. "You can't prove it one way or another."

Olivia had seen Mario's spaced-out look before, one eyebrow raised, his face motionless. "What are you thinking?"

After a long hesitation, he replied, "I'll convince Jay it matched." His eyes were intense, looking at the ceiling, and his arms were resting on the back of his head. "Let's see where it takes us."

The Royal Street Grocery was three blocks away. It was a beautiful day for a walk but Mario opted to take his car. A hunch Jay might be his man for the murder, and a car would be needed for transporting him to Central Lockup. Mario parked on the side street of the grocery, not to give notice that a cop was entering. It didn't matter, as his suit and tie were a quick giveaway that he wasn't a French Quarter local or tourist.

He flashed his badge at the only cashier at the front when he entered the small and smelly grocery. It was crawfish season and a fresh boil had just been pulled from the pot to cool. The robust blend of seasoning consumed the building from the rear of the store all the way to the front door. Mario was directed to the produce section, where he found Jay bent over a crate of apples, placing them carefully on display. As expected, he appeared nervous when Mario came from behind.

"Detective?"

Mario picked up on Jay's eyes roaming, as if there was a squad of police to arrest him. Jay's nervousness spread, and he dropped two apples on the floor.

For a split-second, Mario got a glimpse of a scared man who looked as if he wanted to run. Encountering, for the second time, a detective investigating a murder intensifies the fright by 1,000 percent. Jay was frightened, his complexion beet red, hands a little shaky, and he wouldn't make eye contact.

Looking guilty, the toothpick wiggled in his mouth. The first interview he'd said it was a bad habit since childhood. Mario's opinion was that the toothpick was a stress mechanism. Based on the wiggling of the wood hanging from his lip, Jay had hit his threshold of coping.

"I wanted to ask a few follow-up questions." Mario watched Jay's actions.

Fiddling with the apples stopped when Jay dropped another one, "Shoot," he said, leaning against the apple box. "What do you want to know?"

"What were you and Leon disputing?"

"What? He was my friend. I had his back, and he had mine for two tours in Iraq."

Mario walked a few feet away to get an angle on Jay, should he make a run. "When you got home, things changed. Didn't they?"

Jay was at the point of shouting. Mario preferred to grab him by the neck and beat the truth out, but letting him rattle on might incriminate him. Jay opened up and explained they'd served eight years in the Army. Leon came home with one arm missing, and both were living on the streets within two years of discharge. Then he stopped talking in midsentence. Emotions took over and a tear ran down his face.

"I'll make you a deal. You walk out with me and take a ride downtown, and I won't cuff you in front of your new boss and friends."

Jay shook his head up and down, took his red logo apron off, and advised his boss he'd be back in an hour.

At the Eighth District station, Mario had Jay locked in a questioning room—a place less intimidating than downtown at Central Lockup. At this point, there was nothing to charge him with, but Mario was sure a confession was forthcoming.

In the office, Howard surfaced and found Mario in the coffee room. When asked how Atlantic City was, he denied being there.

He winked. "That problem between you and that guy in AC?"

Mario looked around, making sure they were alone. "Yeah."

"It's over. There's been a change of heart." Howard grabbed a cup of coffee and stopped at the door. "You coming?"

"You better give me more than that," Mario demanded and stepped to catch up.

"All I can say—sleep well; it's over."

Howard entered the room with a sandwich and a Coke from the vending machine. "Nice to see you again, Jay."

Jay's nervousness came back. "Do I need a lawyer?"

"I don't know. Do you?"

He was frightened and expressed he might be in trouble, possibly best to have an attorney. Mario suggested he hear him out first and decide later if he wanted an attorney.

From a folder, Mario pulled a picture of Leon's lifeless body lying in the weeds. Grossed, Jay turned away. Howard insisted he looked carefully at the photo.

A closeup of Leon's head showed a single bullet in his forehead.

"It's a point-blank shot." Howard forced him to look. "No more than four feet away."

Mario chimed in. "The shooter knew both Leon and Barry to get this close."

Jay sat silent. His eyes looked everywhere but at the detectives. Mario gave Howard a slight nod. Howard picked up on the hint. All Mario had left was to outright accuse Jay of shooting Leon and Barry. However, Jay's reaction wasn't at all what the detectives expected when he reached for the pictures.

"How could he have done this?" Jay sat, physically shaking. "After all they had been through and then to die on their own home soil. It's awful."

"Who's he?" Mario asked. "Come on, Jay, you know something."

Howard saw compassion in Jay's eyes. He was heart-wrenchingly sad and loved these guys. The three, like many other veterans, had been to hell and back. Coming home was questionable for some survivors of war. They would rather die in battle than to be killed at home, senselessly.

"Come on, Jay." Howard sat at the end of the table next to Jay. One foot resting on the floor. "For the love of your Army buddies—let us help."

"Help!" Rebounded from the walls. "No one can help me or protect me from this monster. Who would kill their own brother?"

Mario reached over the table and held Jay by the hands.

"I will protect you—I promise. Did Wallace Jackson kill his brother?"

It seemed like forever. Finally his head shook up and down. "Yes."

It took an hour to calm him down, which gave them time to get the DA's attorney, Pamela Jones, to the office with a camera crew. He was in a secure room, where no one else could see through one-way glass or turn a mic on to hear Jay's statement. Immediately after, he'd be escorted by US Marshals to an undisclosed, secure destination until trial. Mario was sure the chief would assist with this substantial proof of the mayor's wrongdoings.

Jay stated his full name, his connection to the two murdered men, and how he was an eyewitness to the murders. He related that Wallace asked Leon to meet him in the park. Barry went along and was to leave when talks started. Barry was mostly there to be a witness that the mayor and Leon met that day. It was a precaution gone wrong. Jay stood back in the weeded area with the camera. Leon wanted more pictures of the meeting. It was early morning. Barry and Leon stood next to a tree when Wallace came up. Barry did his part and started to walk away. The mayor pulled him back by the arm and did the talking. Shortly after, he pulled a gun out and shot them both.

"Barry was shot first, as he was closer, then Leon. The gun had a silencer; when fired, it sounded like a champagne cork." Jay was deep into the brush and saw the whole thing.

Mario identified himself on camera as the detective in charge of the investigation. When Jay was asked if there was anything else he could add, his eyes shifted. Mario pushed for more to the point that Pamela stopped the filming.

"You can't badger a witness and expect a judge to hand down an indictment," she said.

Mario pressured Jay off camera that if he had more to share, now was the time to let it flow. They had enough information to accuse Mayor Wallace Jackson. For the charges to stick was something else to consider. The DA would want more to put his name and job on the line. Without solid proof from someone other than a homeless wino, any reasonably talented attorney would rip the DA apart in court. For now, Pamela would go back and test the waters with her boss.

Mario told Pamela to sit tight while they moved Jay to another room. Pamela and her assistant flopped on a chair out of frustration. It was a waiting game when gathering information for a case. Especially one as delicate as putting the mayor of New Orleans behind bars for life.

In a private office, Jay came through like a champ. Without video and other people around, he confided more in Mario and Howard. Jay said that he took two pictures of the meeting with the mayor. When an uproar started and the mayor pulled a weapon, he snapped a picture. The undeveloped film was still in a camera, hidden, if the heat hadn't destroyed it yet.

Mario was stopped, as he took Jay by the arm to escort him to the camera. Jay had more.

"I followed Wallace back to city hall. I can show you where he dropped the silencer in a street drain and the gun in another."

It hadn't rained in a few days and both items were heavy, so Howard was sure they would still be in place. "They should be in the drain within a few feet of street level."

Jay was taken back into the room, and his testimony was videotaped. Then they were off to find the evidence.

Only the two detectives, Pamela, and her camera person knew what was going on. However, Mario took no chances. Two police units tailed him to the camera. In an alley, Jay had hidden the camera within the same block as Leon hid the photos. There was no problem—the camera was stashed behind bricks and it had been kept cool during the day.

Then, they were off to Lafayette Square where they walked, with the patrol cars following. At a street drain Jay pointed out, Mario marked a red X with a can of spray paint. Around the corner, Jay stopped at another pipe, and an X was painted. Mario was sure Jay was telling the truth. He had no hesitation at pointing out the locations. Jay explained how he remembered the drains by the landmark storefronts.

Mario scanned the area of each drain, up and down the street. "The slick bastard knew these side streets didn't have cameras."

Howard smiled. "Does it matter? This asshole is going down."

CHAPTER 30

JAY SPENT THE NIGHT at Big Gabe's house with Cyrus and three cops. It was all that could be done until a judge issued a subpoena. Before that happened, the DA needed the facts.

At five the next morning, a call went out to the Sewerage and Water Board supervisor of the city. There was one person on duty overnight in case a fire hydrant got knocked out by a car accident. In that case, a crew would need to be called before the streets flooded and water pressure dropped in the neighborhood. This was different. Gary Nicholes was on duty and requested a three-man team to meet the police at Camp Street at the back of Lafayette Square. The utility truck and the crew followed Mario's car to the two street drains marked with a red X.

Mario's car blocked the area. A road sign was set up that showed "Men at Work," and orange cones were placed to block off this section of Camp Street. One man watched for traffic, while one man used a crowbar to lift the manhole cover. Another worker climbed down the ladder into the underbelly of the streets of New Orleans and searched for the weapon. He raked through the trash and found nothing.

Gary explained to Mario that from the street drain, there was a drop of four feet to a catch basin under the street. If the gun were found, it would be in the bowl. If it went farther, there was no way of finding the weapon. It could be hundreds of feet underground.

Mario pointed out that it had not rained in days, so there was nothing to wash the weapon any farther. Gary made a phone call to the head of sanitation. The man in charge confirmed that twice a week, a street-cleaning truck washed the roads. Significant water pressure forced trash through the drains into catch basins to keep the pipes open.

"The street was washed last night," Gary said.

"We need to catch a break." Mario looked down into the hole and waited.

From down below, a muffled voice shouted, "I might have something." The man surfaced with a piece of steel held by his gloved fingers.

Mario held a plastic bag open. "Yes, it's the silencer." It was dropped into the bag and tagged for evidence.

The process was moved to the next drain at the corner of Camp and Poydras Streets. Within fifteen minutes, the gun was recovered.

Mario headed directly to Olivia's research laboratory, where she had been at work since early morning. A light over the door glowed red, so he waited. Through the glass, Mario saw Olivia come through a door and the red light went out.

"Anything?" Mario shouted, before Olivia opened the door.

"Not what you were hoping for." She took her protective eye shield off. In hand were two pictures, held by a clip, still wet with photo-developing fluid. "Both show Wallace standing to the side of Leon and Barry. But, no gun is visible."

"Another picture of the meeting?" Mario gave a head shake and handed her the plastic bag. "The gun pieces were exactly where Wallace dropped them."

"Should be all we need." Olivia took the evidence to process.

Mario waited at her desk for a report about fingerprints on the weapons. His phone vibrated in his coat pocket. "Hello?"

It was Howard. He was at the Royal Street newsstand standing curbside with a New York Times newspaper. One of the few places in the city that carried out-of-state papers. The headlines were read to Mario. "New Jersey Mob Boss Roberto Ferrari Missing." The article stated the information was reported by Roberto's longtime associate, Bobby Galeffi.

"You're telling me Roberto is dead?"

"Let's leave it as—Roberto is out of your life forever."

Mario sat back in a chair. If Howard had played a part in the disappearance of Roberto, he didn't want to know, but it was a significant weight off his mind.

Olivia rushed back to her desk and typed in something on her computer. "Look at this." She pointed at the monitor. The gun and the silencer lay on a white cloth.

Mario viewed it. "What am I looking at?"

"Nothing," Olivia said, swinging her chair around. "Not one print on either piece."

"You've got to be wrong."

"I checked twice." Olivia pulled her glasses off. "They're clean."

"Then the gun doesn't mean crap." Mario rubbed his hand through his hair. "It's just a gun found in the drain. Could have been involved in any one of hundreds of murders in the city."

There was nothing left to do but present the evidence to District Attorney Gilbert James. Mario called ahead, and Pamela Jones met him in the lobby. The DA agreed to see them on short notice, and they were set up in a conference room. Gilbert was at the head of the table. Mario laid out the details. Pictures of the mayor meeting Leon and passing what looked like money. The videotape of Jay's statement ran twice. Photographs of the gun and the silencer. A final picture of Wallace meeting Leon and Barry within an hour of their deaths.

Gilbert James was a man of few words. He always got to the point and quickly. "I'll have to sit on this overnight."

Mario reminded him that Jay's life was in danger without being in protective custody.

"Pamela," Gilbert said, "can you make a case with one witness? A homeless guy?"

"He's a decorated soldier with an honorable discharge. I'll focus on the positive."

Gilbert rubbed his face. "Sure, and the defense will focus on what he's done for the last few years. A drunk living on the streets." Both hands brushed over his face.

Mario gave a side glance at Pamela. She frowned. It wasn't the enthusiasm he'd wanted.

"Any judge will throw out the gun," Gilbert said. "It has no connection to the case. Nothing more than a gun found in an underground water drain."

Gilbert reached for a photo of Wallace slipping Leon something. He referred to the claim that Leon was a half-brother of Wallace. If it were money he handed off, the defense would say there was nothing wrong with giving a handout to his brother.

Mario's beeper vibrated on his belt. On the screen, it read "Olivia 911," a code for him to call immediately. He excused himself and walked into the hallway and called her.

She answered on the first ring. "Bad news. It's not the gun."

"What do you mean?" Mario shot back.

"The bullets we pulled out of Barry and Leon didn't come from this gun."

"What the hell?" Mario said, loud enough to turn heads in the hallway.

Mario went back to the conference room in time for Gilbert to say, "I'll sleep on it and have an answer in the morning."

"Sir, it might be best for me to get you some additional information," Mario said. Getting a horrible side glance from Pamela. "No need to bother, let me work on it further."

Mario left the meeting with Pamela close on his heels. Once clearly in the lobby, she let him have it with both barrels. She quickly cooled her heels when told they didn't have a case.

A call to Howard with the gun situation overshadowed the good news of Roberto's death. They agreed to meet at Big Gabe's Car Wash and revisit Jay. On the way, Mario made a side trip to talk to some homeless people under the Claiborne Avenue bridge.

When Mario arrived at the car wash, Howard's car was being detailed, courtesy of Gabe any time his guys had time. They didn't touch Mario's car. One, it was too dirty inside. Some said he ate every meal in his car. But most of all, he had too many guns in the trunk.

Mario was fired up and double-stepped to the rear of the house. He called off the two cops protecting the front of the building and the one guarding the house.

Hearing the cops were dismissed, Jay voiced, "What the hell?! I gave up information that could get me killed."

"No! You gave me a bunch of bullshit," Mario shouted. "And you better start telling me the truth." He was gambling but had a decent hunch. Then his pager went off again with the same code to call Olivia.

He walked around to what Big Gabe called his courtyard. It was nothing more than overgrown weeds, but Gabe liked to pretend. "What do you have?"

"We have a winner," she said.

"That mother—"

He returned to the kitchen where Jay sat at the table with Howard's leg across the doorway. Cyrus was over the stove making eggs as fast as he could. The kitchen was heating up, and it wasn't from the stove.

Mario came in, smiling, asking for help. How could the gun in the drain not match the bullets in the two dead guys?

He danced around for a few seconds, then grabbed Jay by the throat and lifted him off the chair.

"Do you think I'm stupid or are you that dumb?" Mario jammed him back into the chair.

"The bullets didn't match the gun in the drain. You sent us on a wild goose chase."

"What are you talking about?" Jay shouted, defending himself. "I watched the mayor shoot them both and drop the pieces in the drains."

Mario pulled his gun, cocked the hammer, and placed it in Jay's mouth. Howard was surprised at such a bold move; he'd used it often, but never seen Mario play that card. "You'll tell me the truth, or I'll blow your head off."

Mario holstered his gun and paced the floor. Cyrus dropped a frying pan in the sink and vacated in a flash.

"Know who I talked to earlier?" Mario circled around and got in Jay's face. "Randy." Then he watched Jay's complexion change from rosy to pale white.

With help, Mario gathered information among the homeless population under the bridge. Randy was a big help in locating Jay's cart, deep in the weeds behind an abandoned car. Jay's worldly possessions in the cart and a gun hidden under all his crap. The ballistics report on Jay's weapon was a decisive match to the pistol that killed Barry. Olivia was processing the bullet that killed Leon.

Fear took over, and Jay sat at the table with his hands to his face. Mario shouted questions he didn't answer. Leaning into him still got no response. Howard made a nod to Mario, and he stepped aside.

"Jay, look at me," Howard said politely but stern.

His tear-soaked face raised from the table.

Howard talked calmly, asking for the truth, assuring him Mario wouldn't have shot him when the gun was placed in his mouth. Then he pulled his weapon and put it to Jay's head. "But, I'll kill you right now. Not here—in the swamp. Leave you there with a bullet in each leg, so you can't walk away. Let the gators feast and disassemble you piece by piece."

Howard picked him up from the neck with one hand and pushed Jay's shaky body to the door. Mario's cell phone rang, interrupting the mood, and he answered.

With the phone to his ear, Mario's eyes widened as he listened. "You're sure?" He threw the phone on the table and motioned for Howard to sit Jay back in a chair.

"You have one chance to tell me everything or you're dead." Mario looked up at Howard. "The bullet that killed Leon didn't come from Jay's gun."

Fifteen minutes later, Jay visibly in pain, rocked back and forth, then finally came clean.

He said that it started over breakfast at the Church of St. Patrick. Barry and Leon argued that it was time to make a payday and extort money from the mayor. Leon didn't agree. Jay was told to stay back; they didn't need pictures of another meeting.

They left breakfast about 6:15 A.M. Jay pushed his cart one way, Leon and Barry walked two blocks over to Lafayette Square. Jay, curious, doubled back and hid in the bushes. When the mayor shouted, waving his hands in the air, Jay snapped a few pictures. Wallace was long gone when Leon and Barry's squabble heated up. Barry stepped away, then quickly turned back with a gun and shot Leon in the head.

Jay rooted through his cart, pulled his gun, the only actual possession he owned and kept for protection on the streets. Barry had bent over Leon, spit on Leon. When he turned around, Jay fired his gun and Barry dropped to the ground.

Jay looked relieved; one hand brushed his hair back. "Leon was my friend. We've been through a lot of bad times together. He didn't deserve to die that way."

"Do you have the gun that Barry used?" Mario spoke in his compassionate voice. Jay was genuinely sorry for his actions.

Jay said he could take them to that gun. The weapon that he planted in the drains was found weeks earlier in the weeds. He was smart enough to know that a gun and a silencer couldn't be pawned without severe repercussions. His plan was to drop them in the river but never got a chance.

"You cleaned the fingerprints and made the drop in the drain yourself?" Howard asked.

Jay nodded his head up and down. With his hands over his face, he whispered, "I should have just run and called the police."

"In the end, you did the right thing," Mario said. "You came clean."

"Will I go to prison?" Jay's eyes widened; his voice escalated. "Leon saved my life in Iraq. I had to kill Barry for taking his life."

"Call it what you want. Murder, giving a false statement

under oath, and obstruction." Mario put handcuffs on him. "Yeah, you're going to jail—for a long time."

CHAPTER 31

"ALL RISE," THE BAILIFF announced when the judge entered the courtroom. On one side up front was Pamela Jones, representing the district attorney's office. Across the aisle were Jay Adams and his attorney. Mario and Howard sat in the back as the arraignment started.

When the judge asked Jay Adams to enter a plea, a man stood. "Gustavo Martino, Your Honor, representing Jay Adams. My client pleads self-defense."

Pamela jumped to her feet. Self-defense was news to her. Only two days ago, he'd confessed to murder. "Your Honor?" The prosecution asked that Jay be held without bail.

"Your Honor, may we approach?" Gustavo said. The judge waved them to the bench. "Sir, not to embarrass Ms. Jones, we agree about the bail. A homeless man welcomes jail, three meals a day, a bed, and a roof over his head. My client is happy in prison for the short term."

The judge motioned them to return to their places and ruled that Jay Adams was to be held without bail and the trial date was set.

Mario was as surprised as anyone, seeing Gustavo and

hearing the plea changed. "What the hell just happened? How did Jay hire the most powerful defense attorney in the entire South?"

Howard rolled his eyes. "Do you think Jay should be sent to prison for life?"

Mario made a face, wrinkled his cheeks. "I'm not sure."

"Well, I don't. With the Savino family dead, Gustavo had room for a new client."

"For gratis?"

"Gustavo does nothing for gratis." Howard rolled his eyes.

The judge moved on to another case, and the detectives took the conversation to the hallway.

It was as if a lightning bolt hit Mario, and he reached for Howard's arm. "Did you use our investment money?"

"You said you wanted to do good with the money." Howard stopped before going down an escalator to the street level. "I don't believe Jay should go to prison."

Mario hated to know but asked anyway. "How much?"

"Gustavo capped his fee at one hundred thousand dollars."

The detectives met with Chief Parks to follow up on Jay's arrest. Mario came clean with the chief about the mayor's investigation. He was told to tread water carefully after the meeting with the district attorney.

"This mayor thing you're pursuing has to come to a head." The chief was emphatic; if the story got out without solid proof, she'd deny it and throw Mario under the bus. There was no way she would take the blame. Her department would look like they operated as a three-ring circus, with Mario as the ringmaster.

Howard insisted Mayor Jackson had ties to a crime boss, and they needed more time to work out the details.

"What proof can possibly come up that the mayor is associated with Roberto? And now the crime boss has gone missing." She gave them an unfriendly look. "I read the New York Times too. Doesn't take a genius to know the one gone missing might be the one associated with the mayor."

Howard kept his eyes down; he knew she was looking at him and Mario too. He was offering information.

"You have a week," she said. "Make a case or move on and never look back at this ridiculous accusation of our city's leader."

Mario and Howard brainstormed over lunch. Howard called Julie and she confirmed that Roberto had not surfaced. One thing she knew for sure—the hit on Mario and Olivia had been called off. When Howard hung the phone up he sat in a daze. Mario spoke, but Howard's mind was far, far away.

"Hello?" Mario said, waving his hand at Howard.

"I have a solution," Howard said. "I'm sure I can nail the mayor." He stood. "I've got to go. I'll be in touch."

"Where are you going?" Mario shouted at his back.

"Just trust me."

"That's what worries me," Mario whispered to himself.

CHAPTER 32

A CALL TO BOBBY G. set up a meeting with Howard at the Philadelphia airport baggage claim area. Bobby assured him that if there was any funny business he'd find himself in the trunk of a car and dumped in a landfill. Death would not be without severe pain. Howard pointed out he was flying commercial, so screening wouldn't allow him to sneak a weapon onboard. He came in peace this trip.

The flight was under three hours. Howard was among the first few off the plane and arrived at the baggage carousel first. He was met by a man in a dark blue suit; red, white, and blue tie; and shiny shoes. No doubt he was an airport employee—on Bobby G's payroll. Why else would he give up his office on the ground floor and look the other way?

Inside, Bobby sat behind a desk, one brute next to him and two thugs at the door. Howard was searched politely—he respected the move.

"I've done what you asked. Mario is a free man," Bobby said. "What now?"

"I'm here to make you a rich man." Howard looked at the bodyguards. "We need to speak alone."

"Not going to happen."

Howard clarified that if they didn't speak alone, he was taking the next flight to New Orleans.

"How rich?' Bobby asked.

"More than your great-grandchildren can blow in a lifetime."

They moved their conversation outside the office, where the sounds echoed through the ground level with announcements and the baggage carousel running. They stood outside the office, and the thugs spread out with eyes glued on Bobby. Howard was sure the thugs had quick access to their guns, if he made any sudden moves.

He watched Bobby's eyes widen as he laid out a plan. He asked if Roberto was ever coming back, suggesting maybe Roberto was on an extended vacation in Italy. With a head shake and a smile, Bobby guaranteed that unless Roberto was reincarnated, he wasn't coming back.

"I'll call you tomorrow," Howard said, shaking Bobby's hand. "I appreciate your cooperation."

Bobby called out, "Mr. Blitz," before Howard got too far. "Maybe this is the start of a beautiful relationship."

"Don't get emotional. I need something from you—it's just business."

After less than an hour on the ground, Howard was back in the air heading to New Orleans. Everything was in place, with one stumbling block facing him. Convincing Mario on the strategy.

The flight back was quick. With no baggage, he was soon in the car and on his way. One call to Mario found him at Olivia's house. Uninvited, he arrived on her front porch. A slight knock, and the door opened to an infuriated Mario. Scents of candles hit him when he walked in the door. "Is that cranberry scent?" He got no acknowledgment. The dining room table was set for two, with good china and crystal wine glasses. No doubt, a romantic dinner was planned.

"Mario, we need to talk."

Making a slight eye motion toward the door, Mario couldn't have thrown a better hint with a head cocked the same direction, "Can't it wait until tomorrow?"

Olivia came in with another place setting. "Of course, it can't wait. He'll have a meal with us, and you two can discuss a case over dinner."

Howard apologized for barging in on their romantic dinner. He didn't mean to ruin the mood and promised he'd only be a few minutes.

Olivia insisted he stay and banged the dishes on the table. "Mood! The mood changed the second you walked through the door."

Mario reached for the wine and poured three glasses. "Guess you're staying for dinner."

Mario asked what was so important. Howard took his wine to the sofa in the living room. He talked fast, and Mario's nod indicated he was in agreement. The second time Olivia shouted that dinner was on the table, Howard took his conversation to the dining room.

Howard looked the spread over. Chicken breast stuffed with wild rice and mushrooms, sautéed vegetables, buttered potatoes, and French rolls. "Haven't seen a spread like this in a long time."

Mario's eyes stabbed at Howard. "It's been a long time for me too pal."

Over dinner, Olivia suggested she introduce Howard to a woman she'd met shopping. Age appropriate for Howard and might help take his mind off work. She said he was worse than Mario.

"How age appropriate?" Howard raised one eyebrow.

Olivia came back with a vengeance. "Your age!"

Dinner was finished. Mario helped take the dishes to the kitchen and before Olivia joined them on the sofa, Howard hit him with the demands. "We can take down a corrupt mayor. All you need to do is endorse the casino—don't go out of your way to dodge it."

"Lie?" Mario said.

"No. Simply say you have no opinion about the casino business."

"But I've been against it from the start." Mario knocked back the rest of his wine.

"Opinions change." Howard walked the room like he was interviewing a witness. "Why care? Let the city officials take the heat if crime spikes."

"You're sure it will work?"

Howard gulped his wine. "I guarantee."

For the plan to work, the chief had to play a part. It wasn't anything that would tie her to Mario's probe into the mayor—so she agreed.

The next day, Chief Parks was to meet Mayor Jackson at his office. She was right on time at 1:45 P.M. She opened with her condolences on his brother's death. He sucked up the sympathy like the two were attached at the hip throughout their lives.

She got her point across and asked the purpose of the meeting. How should the police spokesperson handle questions from the press regarding Leon Mason? She was surprised to learn the mayor had called for a press conference that evening.

Across town at One Shell Square, Mario and Howard sat listening on speakerphone in Ralph's office. He agreed to use his computer hacking knowledge to frame Wallace Jackson.

Ralph walked Bobby G. through instructions on Roberto Ferrari's laptop. It took three tries but Ralph finally had control of Roberto's computer.

"I'm in," Ralph said. "Okay, Bobby, don't touch any keys." Then Ralph opened Roberto's email account and transferred all his sent files to his computer. Ralph located a folder named "Gaming New Orleans." "Holy shit! We hit the motherlode." There were hundreds of emails back and forth between Roberto and the mayor.

From Roberto's mirrored computer, an email was sent to the mayor. By now, the chief would have been gone from their meeting, and the mayor, in his office, would be able to respond. Her job was to make sure the mayor was at his desk when Ralph shot off the first email.

Wallace received an email alert on his phone that his personal account had new mail. He pulled it up and read.

SENT: Roberto Ferrari

I'm alive and well. Need to be out of the country for a while. Are we still in business?

At Ralph's office, Mario and Howard watched the inbox for the mayor to respond. It was a waiting game and finally a bell sounded, showing a response.

SENT: Wallace Jackson

A stroke of my pen and you'll have my recommendation as a vendor for the casino licensee. Gaming Control Board will approve. I appointed every decision-maker.

Mario handed Ralph a handwritten note for a reply to Wallace. "Send it—every word."

Ralph reviewed the information and typed the message with some hesitation. He might get into a gray area, and if Wallace caught it, he'd know this was a setup. He wanted to review some of the previous emails to get a feel for Roberto's style. Mario stressed it would happen now or never. This had one shot in a million of working and it had to be now.

SENT: Roberto Ferrari

I'm ready! Advise day, time, location, and amount.

They waited for a response. It didn't come back as fast as the first one. Mario flipped from looking at the screen to Ralph's fingers, typing and clicking away. He had no clue what he was doing.

"Come on," Ralph said, annoyed, beating on the desk like that would help the computer search faster. "Wallace isn't responding. I'm searching the email folder for 'street, avenue, road, or boulevard,' some clue to lead me to an email with the amount and location."

"He's onto us," Howard said. "He should have answered by now."

A bell sounded; an email was in the inbox.

SENT: Wallace Jackson

Sorry, I was interrupted. Tomorrow, 3:00 P.M. Same location and amount.

"We're screwed," Ralph said.

"Buy time," Mario shouted.

SENT: Roberto Ferrari

Okay.

The search for "avenue" came back "no match" and so did the other keywords.

Mario walked the room a little faster than usual. "What else can a street be called?"

"I can't think straight," Ralph said, gawking out the window for the answer.

Howard suggested the word "lane." As fast as it was typed "no match" came back.

"Try 'circle,'" Mario said.

"Oh, my god. We got it." Ralph opened an email from eight months ago. It read they were to meet at the House of God on Lee Circle. "It just says to bring the cash."

Mario made a crazy face. The money didn't matter, just a location for the drop.

Wallace had incriminated himself in the email. Now they needed a legal search and to catch him in the act.

CHAPTER 33

THROUGH THE NIGHT RALPH printed off every email between Wallace and Roberto. It was an assembly line. Ralph printed the emails. Mario and Howard with white gloves took the emails and read through circling in red anything that could be used in court.

Mario walked the room like a high-powered attorney in a murder trial. "Can the ink on the emails be traced?"

"Sure, it's an HP laser printer," Ralph said. "Might take a while, probably fifty thousand in the city."

"So the answer is no." Mario paced more.

Howard circled an entire paragraph and passed it to Mario. All the answers were found in one email instructing Roberto to make the drop at the House of God on Lee Circle, Ignatius Green's church.

"Holy crap!" Mario said. "The mayor's campaign is funded with a payoff from the mob through donations to the church. Pastor Green is the bag man."

Daylight broke through the window, making them realize they had worked through the night. Coffee, breakfast, and a shower were needed by all before they could package a solid case to present to District Attorney Gilbert James.

Mario was preparing to leave when Ralph reminded him of an appointment to see a house that afternoon. Knowing Mario was busy with the mayor issue, Ralph suggested he'd go alone and take pictures. Mario agreed.

"You're buying a house?" Howard asked, as the elevator expressed to the lobby.

"Maybe," Mario said.

After a quick shower, the detectives met at an IHOP for a stack of pancakes. Mario called the chief and was to meet her within an hour. It would all depend on him selling her on the takedown of the mayor. Without the chief's support, Gilbert wouldn't consider the information coming from Mario a second time.

They hashed over an idea and agreed it could work. A stop at Gustavo Martino's office started the plan in motion. He saw them without an appointment.

There wasn't a lot of time, so Howard let Mario do all the talking. Gustavo sat back in his chair, all ears, his hands in prayer mode under his chin. Mario was sure the information was being considered.

Gustavo stood, came around the front of his desk, and leaned into Mario's face. "Something doesn't smell right. You put the fee up for Jay, and now you want to cut a deal to get him off with no time served?"

"Self-defense," Mario said.

Gustavo laughed. "I have to sell the jury on it first."

"My way, you don't even have to go to court." Mario got eye to eye with him. "And you get to keep a big fat fee for doing just about nothing."

"That's my point. It smells like a setup. Maybe get me on corruption?"

Mario was losing the battle. They'd hated each other for years. He'd lock gangsters up, and Gustavo would do what high-powered attorneys did—confuse the jury until there was reasonable doubt. His clients never served time.

Silence hung over the room.

"You can talk to my client, but I'm going to be present."

Mario agreed, and they were off to Central Lockup.

Jay came down to the interview room in shackles and was released to the detectives. Gustavo asked for the handcuffs to be removed, but the guard refused. The room was private with a guard stationed outside the door.

Mario kept his voice just above a whisper. His opening words got Jay's attention. "I have a way for you to walk out of here a free man."

Jay didn't have to reply. His eyes sparkled with a willingness to follow Mario's directions. Once the plan was discussed, Jay agreed to have his statement on film and signed an agreement.

In the end, Gustavo shook Mario's hand. "You must really believe in this guy."

Mario gave a nod. "Sometimes you have to revert to street justice."

On the way to police headquarters, Howard came up with an idea. Mario moved on it quickly and called Ralph. A second copy of the emails was printed, except for the dialog between Wallace and who he thought was Roberto the day before.

On the way to police headquarters, Mario pulled

curbside at One Shell Square and met Ralph. He handed Mario a greasy, stained Burger King bag and off Mario went to see the chief.

Jay's statement was short, but to the point, and it was all the chief needed to hear. She pulled a few emails from the nasty Burger King bag and read them. Then she buzzed her assistant. "Call Gilbert James. Tell him to make himself available—I'm on my way."

"Yes, madam chief," she replied.

She would give the DA a chance to decide, if not her next stop was the attorney general.

Gilbert reviewed the video, looked through the emails, and leaned back in his chair. Mario looked at his watch and peeked at Howard. Time was running out, and they had to make a move for this to play out positively for Jay.

"Let me be clear in my understanding." Gilbert pulled his chair closer to the desk. "Leon Mason gave these emails to Jay to hold."

"Correct," Mario replied.

"But we don't know how Leon got them."

"Doesn't matter," Mario said straight-faced. "The emails are time-stamped and incriminating to both Roberto Ferrari and Wallace Jackson."

"And how did this come about?"

"Gustavo learned about it while prepping his client and called me," Mario said.

"Gustavo. There's no love between him and this office."

"I know, sir," Howard spoke up. "I'm not a fan either. Jay directed us to the Burger King bag—it was recovered in the exact location he testified."

Gilbert stood looking out the window at downtown New Orleans. Nothing said was a good sign that meant he was considering. He pulled a few sheets of coffee-stained emails from the bag.

Mario didn't dare look at Howard. He was sure Howard thought the same. Ralph had done a great job making the paper look worn and like it had been stashed in a damp hiding place for some time.

"Gustavo is demanding leniency for his client, Jay Adams," Mario said.

"If it leads to the arrest of the mayor, I'll consider." He threw the papers back into the nasty bag. "What do you want from me?"

Those were the magic words Mario had waited to hear. "I need a court order for the host to turn over all communications from Mayor Jackson's personal emails."

Gilbert directed Pamela Jones to go with the paperwork in hand to the judge's chambers for a signature. The detectives followed Pamela and snatched the signed subpoena from her hands when she stepped out of the judge's chambers.

"Thank you!" Mario said, all but running to the car.

They arrived at Olivia's office with the subpoena for her to start the process. The procedure was slow and based on the cooperation of the email provider. The DA's request was for all correspondence in the last sixty days. Olivia's experience working with providers for that much information would take a week or more for the results.

Mario's expression indicated he didn't have time to wait.

She asked, "What do you want from me?"

"Your friend at the FBI," Mario said. "I need an email the mayor sent yesterday."

"Only one?" she asked with some question in her mind. "Sounds like you already know what's in the correspondence."

"Olivia!" he said, head down gathering his thoughts for the correct way to phrase his request. "I don't have time for fifty questions. Make the call."

She huffed and mumbled under her breath, "You always need things done—in a hurry. Get a cup of coffee. I'll have something for you before you're finished."

The detectives followed her direction and took a seat in the breakroom. It wasn't the best coffee, but caffeine was needed by both. They sipped and watched the clock tick. Time wasn't on their side, the rendezvous for the money drop was fast approaching.

As promised, Olivia returned quickly with three emails between Mayor Jackson and Roberto Ferrari. "I'm not going to ask how you knew about these emails."

"Good, then don't," he said.

With the evidence in hand, he and Howard rushed back to headquarters and presented the findings to the chief. It was a long process to get to the same point they were at eighteen hours earlier, but now everything was legal and would hold up in court.

The chief ordered fifty thousand in cash from the evidence room, packaged in a small canvas bag. She agreed to Mario's suggestion of a bag man. An undercover agent, Nico Dimitriou, a long-time police officer, was selected.

He pulled off being an Italian mob guy despite his Greek heritage. He was briefed as fast as Mario could talk on every possible question that might be asked of Roberto's bag man.

Nico was fitted for a mic. An argument broke out when the chief wanted to use a bulky police monitor taped to his inner thigh. Nico made some remark that the equipment was as old as the chief and if searched it'd kill him.

The quarreling continued, and Mario stepped in. "I don't care what device you use, but we have to go—now."

Nico put his coat on, holstered his gun, and grabbed the bag of money.

"What the hell," Chief Parks said. "You walking in with a piece strapped to your chest?"

"I'm a wise guy. I'm expected to have a weapon." She got a nasty look from him.

They had fifteen minutes to get to Lee Circle. The DA was already in place with police backup.

In the parking garage, Nico got in a town car that Howard supplied. He played the part excellently.

The chief leaned into Mario's car window. "How the hell did you come up with the email—so quickly?"

"Olivia ran yesterday's emails between Roberto and Wallace." Mario didn't blink.

"That's my point. How did you pull out of your ass to look at those emails? Why not a week ago, a month, why yesterday?"

"Lucky guess," Mario said, and stepped on the gas.

CHAPTER 34

At 3:03 P.M., Nico walked up to the steps of the House of God carrying the canvas bag. It was an impressive house of worship that Pastor Green had built from a tiny, four-pew, wood structure in New Orleans twenty-five years ago. He was met by a man who appeared to expect him. Nico thought, big son-of-a-bitch. A broke ex-football player working to intimidate for a payday. Didn't matter. Nico had already determined how to take him down when the guy favored his right knee.

"I'm Nico. Roberto sent me."

Across the street, the surveillance team, Mario, and Howard listened in. A thumbs-up between the detectives brought a smile. It had been a long struggle to this point.

"I'll take it from here," the man said, reaching for the bag.

The sting was calculated, down to every possible response. Nico pulled a picture of Pastor Green from his coat.

"Are you Ignatius Green?" Nico asked, with the picture in the guy's face. "Don't look like him. I'll see Ignatius, or I walk. And the donation goes with me."

He made an angry face. Behind a closed door for a minute, then he opened it and waved Nico through. Inside was another big guy and behind a desk was Ignatius Green.

Draped in an expensive suit, a gold Rolex extended beyond the shirt cuff purposely. It was apparent he preached that "the more you give, the more you receive."

"Nico, don't be offended," Ignatius said, with a nod at the two men.

His jacket was taken off, gun removed. Apparently the weapon didn't bother them. Frisked up one leg and down the other. Then Ignatius gave another hand motion to his men and his shirt was neatly unbuttoned.

Nico alerted his team. "You think I'd put a mic on my chest?"

In the truck, Mario got everyone prepared and moved some foot cops closer to the front of the church.

Nico stood, shirt blowing open from the air-conditioning vent overhead.

"What are you looking for?" Nico put them on the defense.

Ignatius was fired up. He said that this was the third drop, and he was pissed that Nico asked to see him directly. The only good part was that if the transmitter was working, he'd just admitted to accepting money twice before.

"Where is Michael Ferrari?" he shouted, slamming his fist on the desk.

In the truck, Mario's head was spinning out of control. "Come on. I told you about Michael. Oh, man! We needed more time to plan this. The wrong answer and Nico's dead."

"With all due respect, pastor, Michael Ferrari was killed about a week ago."

Mario's heart went back to regular repetitions.

"I knew Michael was dead. I just didn't know who you were." Ignatius motioned for Nico's shirt to come off. "Maybe you're a cop."

Nico held his arms up. "Hold on, I didn't know it was that kind of meeting. Here, let me help." Nico took his shirt off and threw it on the desk. Then he unbuckled his belt and dropped his pants to the floor.

In the truck, Mario took a breather. "Thank Christ, the chief didn't win the mic fight."

"Where the hell is it?" Howard asked.

"Inside his belt. He insisted on using his equipment or he'd not do the sting."

Nico got dressed, put his holster back on, and tucked in his shirt. He threw the bag on the desk. "Count the money. Somehow you don't look like the trusting type."

Back in the truck, Howard was waiting for the word to send in the troops and make an arrest. Mario held off giving the go-ahead—he'd like more to seal Ignatius's involvement.

"Who cares how much is in the bag? A donation is never questioned," Ignatius said, but unzipped the bag anyway. A peek inside and he fingered through the bundles. "Is this a joke?"

An uneasiness came over Nico. He was told that the money wasn't going to be an issue. "What's the problem?"

"Ten, short-stack bundles," Ignatius's eyes lifted. "Fifty grand wasn't the agreement."

Nico had him talking. It was dangerous if he ran with his guy—he did anyway. "It's all Roberto is willing to pay."

In the surveillance van, Howard pushed. "Let's take him down. You said yourself the amount didn't matter"

Mario waved him off. "The preacher is about to dig himself a deeper hole."

Then Ignatius blew up. "The final payment was to be one hundred thousand dollars."

"Take it up with Roberto."

Ignatius pulled a gun from his desk drawer. "Or maybe you took out a little taste for yourself."

Nico spoke loudly, making sure the mic picked up every word, "No need for a gun, pastor."

"We have enough." Mario reached for his radio. "Take him down."

Without hesitation, a SWAT team of four entered the church. With high-powered rifles extended, they scanned their path and converged on the back office and took down Pastor Ignatius Green and his two bodyguards.

At city hall, District Attorney Gilbert James and Chief Parks made a career decision and arrested Mayor Wallace Jackson in a city council meeting. He didn't go willingly.

CHAPTER 35

TWO WEEKS LATER WALLACE Jackson was back in court with his attorney, who wasn't Gustavo Martino, his first choice. When Gustavo was contacted, Wallace was told it would be a conflict of interest for him to take on the ex-mayor's case. A promise Gustavo made when Mario laid out the plan to take down the mayor. The last thing Mario wanted was for Wallace to hire the number-one trial attorney in the South. He'd have to settle for number two, but most attorneys and judges felt no one was a close second. No one could match trial banter, confuse the English languish, take the untruths and make them believable, and jumble the jurors' minds into reasonable doubt better than Gustavo.

Mario and Howard stood in the back of the packed courtroom and watched the circus unfold. The room filled with media, supporters, and haters. The hatred carried by many represented years of corrupt politicians in a city they loved.

The judge threw out the request by a team of lawyers representing Wallace to suppress the last email sent by Roberto. Roberto was dead at the time, and the email should not be allowed in evidence.

The judge's speech was brief and covered facts about organized crime leaders. There's always someone in line to take over if a mafia boss goes down. It didn't matter who Wallace thought he was dealing with, Wallace acted and followed through with obstruction of justice and taking a bribe to favor a city contract. Ordering the bomb that killed Truman was an additional charge by the FBI and would be heard in federal court. It was just the beginning of legal problems for the former mayor.

"The emails will stay in as evidence," the judge said, and slammed his gavel.

The same day, on the courthouse steps, Gustavo Martino held a press conference with his client, Jay Adams. He thanked DA Gilbert James for reviewing new information brought forward proving Jay had acted in self-defense in the shooting that took Barry's life. Jay was a free man.

Mario and Howard watched from the bottom of the steps behind cameras, listening to Gustavo Martino grandstand. It was no doubt a satisfying moment to see Jay walk and the real criminal, Wallace Jackson, fight for his life.

Wallace Jackson received perks for his testimony. He said that he paid Leon Mason to only set a smoke bomb under Mario's car to scare him. There was no intent on his part to kill anyone. The tactic was meant to get Mario's attention and have him stop fighting the casino bill, which Wallace desperately needed. It was Leon who decided to mix the chemicals to cause a small fire that should have given the driver time to get out, so he said, when he planted the device. The result of Truman Burnett's death was devastating to Wallace, and he even let a few tears show during the testimony.

The DA went along with the deceitful statement. It closed the case on Truman, and Wallace would never see the outside of a jail for the rest of his life anyway.

In New Orleans, the vice mayor was automatically put in place as acting mayor until the end of the year. In November, an election would be held to vote in a mayor for a four-year term.

Much like the vice president of the United States steps in immediately if the president cannot perform his duties, Garrett Chadwick was sworn in as mayor of New Orleans. Garrett had had his eye on city hall for a few years but was too young to gain the popular vote. But he was smart enough to persuade Wallace Jackson that he was the best person to be his second in command. Wallace, a politician all his life, appointed Garrett as an undeveloped candidate who would be no threat to Wallace for eight years. He planned to be re-elected and didn't care who would run for mayor after he was out of office.

Wallace was wrong, and the guy he called "kid" in a meeting now had the top job in the city. He planned to be elected as mayor when the November elections rolled around.

Garrett knew about the problems that Mario and Wallace had over the casinos. Unlike the former mayor, Garrett had the people of the city at heart. His push was for more jobs, higher wages, tax revenues, road repairs, and economic development.

Three days after taking office, Garrett called a meeting with Mario at Ruth's Chris Steak House. It was the building where politicians and powerbrokers cut deals over red wine and rare meat. It was the best-dressed place in town for lunch, filled with lawyers, judges, members of the city council, and anyone else with a high-paying job and an expense account.

It was the new mayor and Mario discussing business over lunch. In contrast to Wallace, Garrett didn't have a sidekick like Kory Barnes who shadowed his every move. He didn't need an assistant, and Garrett released him the day he took office.

Mario had met Garrett once or twice at award events, and it was nothing more than, "How about them Saints?" Today was different; having the mayor on his side was suitable for his career, providing he proved to be good for the city.

They ordered lunch and Garrett cut to the chase. He defended himself as a twenty-eight-year-old politician with people's conception that he was too green behind the ears to run a city of this size. Some journalists had already branded him "The Mayberry Mayor" and written that he should go get some experience before tackling New Orleans.

Mario listened to him talk nonstop through salads and sizzling filet mignons they both ordered. Garrett covered how he grew up in the city, went to local high schools and colleges, and graduated top of his class. He also worked his way through the family business of a chain of supermarkets and shopping centers. His grandfather, a multimillionaire since an early age, always bolstered him by saying, "If the city were run like a business—we would all benefit."

Mario ate part of his steak and told Garrett to start on his and take a breather. Then hit him with a question. "What do you want from me?"

Garrett threw a hunk of meat in his mouth. "What's your view on the casino project?"

Mario repeated what he had told a reporter before his comments were picked up by every news network in the city. It became a battle when Wallace demanded the police chief to curb Mario's views regarding the town. From that point, it was personal. "My true concern. I fear casinos bring crime. And we don't have the police force to deal with more crime."

"Fair assumption."

Garrett pulled a piece of paper from his coat and glanced down at a list of written items. With the tax money from gambling, he planned to increase the police department with additional manpower, for better protection and traffic flow. The tax dollars would increase teacher's pay in public schools and bring programs to the city to help people out of poverty by creating new jobs.

"Mr. Mayor," Mario said, pushing his plate toward the waiter. "A lot of promises are made, but few are ever carried through."

"If I'm elected this fall, one year after the casino opening, every promise I make will be fulfilled or I'll step down. I need you to go on record that casinos are good for the city, based on my plan." Garrett waited for a reply.

"Why me?"

"Because you have had a strong voice within the community against this bill." Garrett took a sip of water. "And rightfully so, based on how Wallace planned to line his pockets."

Garrett planned to ask the city council for money to run ads in newspapers and on TV about the positive aspects of casino gambling.

"Mr. Mayor," Mario stood. "Thank you for lunch. If you believe this is good for all citizens of New Orleans—I'll back you and put the word out."

"Thank you. Now I'm going over to that table," he said, pointing at four gentlemen. "Those four men sit on the city council. They voted my ad campaign down, so I need to change their minds."

Before Mario left, he asked one more question. The city had already approved gambling; the mayor had only to assign the license to any of six applicants the Gaming Control Board found suitable. The answer wasn't what he expected. Garrett wanted the approval of the people. They needed to believe in his decisions that all his actions were for the best of everyone's interest and the growth of the city and the future.

Mario walked away encouraged, a different feeling of how great it was for a mayor to have the city at heart and what he might do if given a chance.

Back at the Eighth District, Mario sat at his desk with Howard, who thumbed through some phone memo slips. Mario's mind wandered to conversations with Mayor Chadwick. Not that he wanted any part of the political machine that ran the city day by day, but his street power and connections could help.

A business card had been in Mario's desk drawer for some time. Not sure why he would keep it or ever need it. It read, Ferrari's Italian Restaurant on the Boardwalk, in red and green ink on white card stock. No doubt Roberto's grandfather gave the colors some thought, they were the same colors used on the Italian flag. The Sicilian family came to this country for a better life, but they never forgot their roots and the love for their country. The grandfather planned to run an Italian restaurant and hoped for the children to follow. Somewhere, they strayed and became the most powerful boss of bosses on the wrong side of the law.

On the back of the card was a handwritten phone number given him by Bobby G. during the last meeting with Howard. Passed on to Mario, as a gesture of good faith and friendship to call if he ever needed anything. Bobby clarified that he meant dinner reservations at the restaurant. That's how the wise guys worked in understated ways. "Call if you ever need anything" meant "I'm here for you." But at what cost was the question.

Mario never questioned Howard on how Roberto disappeared and why the hit on his own life was cancelled. Grateful, but he preferred not to know the details. Howard went to extremes in his defense, like he was back in the Special Forces for his country and assigned an assassination. His record still held at 100 percent, always hitting his target.

Mario gave a nod and Howard made the call on a throwaway cell phone. Bobby G. answered the call himself.

"Mr. G?" Howard said. "I have someone wanting to talk to you."

Few people had the cell number direct to Bobby. It wasn't out of friendship that Bobby needed a man like Howard on his side. One who got close enough to take him out and would do it again if necessary. Bobby wanted Howard as a friend.

"Bobby G? I need a truthful answer." Mario got directly to the point. "Roberto is gone. Are you the man in charge?"

There was no hesitation. "I am. What do you need?"

CHAPTER 36

TWO DAYS LATER, MARIO and Howard sat in the back seat of a limousine parked on the side of a rusty fence. A roar overhead shook the car as a private jet landed on the north-south runway. The plane taxied, then stopped near the car. The electric stairway came from the belly of the plane and rested on the ground. First to walk off the aircraft was Julie Wong. A man stood at the top of the steps, scanned the area, then waved Bobby G. out of the plane. They all met in the back seat of the limousine.

Mario simplified the details of the casino contract the mayor would issue within a week. If Bobby followed Mario's suggestions, his company would be the sole distributor of food, liquor, and paper products to the New Orleans casinos. A deal worth, on the low side, one hundred million dollars in revenue a year.

Mario would make the introduction of Bobby's "Meat Packing Company and Food Distributors" to Mayor Chadwick. In return, Bobby would grant one favor. A strange look came over Julie. Even she was taken aback with such a request to a mob boss.

It would be easy for Mario to convince Mayor Chadwick

of the plan. Put the East Coast Meat Packing Company and Food Distributors into the deal when awarding the casino licenses. No companies would be fighting for a "cash cow" casino permit, if the city directed what company to buy from, as long as the quality and price were a value.

The feather in the mayor's cap was a guaranteed drug-free city. Garrett believed in Mario, and if he could show force against drug traffickers and stop the drug epidemic without increasing payroll for hundreds of cops to do the job—he was in.

Bobby thought about Mario's proposal longer than expected. His eyes shifted to Howard, Julie, and out the window.

Howard gave him a nod. "Your chance to be one hundred percent legit in New Orleans. Who knows what the future will bring?"

"At what cost?" Bobby asked. "You want me to tell the cartel—New Orleans is off limits."

"You have the power," Mario said. "You're not cutting their distribution. You'll give them more by allowing them into your East Coast cities."

"And why would I do that?"

"To gain the casino business," Mario quickly shot back. "You'll gain new friends who will look up to you for your accomplishments in creating jobs—not fear you for who you are. And, at the same time, you'll earn millions of dollars."

It had been a long-standing agreement that the cartel had foot soldiers on the ground in many Southern cities, New Orleans being one them. Bobby would offer a larger

East Coast city in exchange for keeping New Orleans drug-free.

"Look at it as a business opportunity for the cartel to increase business," Howard added. "Just not in our city."

Bobby made a face. "And if I don't?"

"Not a problem," Mario said, as cold as a twenty-five-pound block of ice.

Bobby cocked his head and motioned, "No repercussions?"

"Oh, I didn't say there wouldn't be consequences." Mario pulled pictures from his pocket. Then rattled off a believable story that the mayor was prepared to train 100 men under the federal government DEA guidelines solely to crack down on drugs coming into the city. He continued with his bullshit story that laws would be passed to prosecute minors as adults if caught selling drugs of any kind or weight.

"It won't be easy to recruit nine- and ten-year-olds to sell drugs when the word gets out." Howard raised an eyebrow. "Minimum five years."

Mario leaned forward, showing a picture of a kid with a backpack standing on a corner. "Think we don't know what the kid has in his backpack?" Another picture, stamped FBI on the back, was put under Bobby's nose. "This little girl—yeah, she looks sweet. She'll sell enough drugs in school to buy a new car. The downside is she'll have to wait four years to get a driver's license. She's twelve!"

"Bobby, the game is over in New Orleans." Howard bent closer and whispered, "You have an out—I advise you to take it."

"Your appointment with the mayor is in thirty minutes," Mario said. "I need an answer."

Mario handed Bobby further instructions needed to close the deal and for him to consider. Bobby and Julie walked back to the aircraft to discuss the options. One of two things would happen: the engines would crank up into a whirlwind of speed and the plane would taxi off or Julie would walk down the steps ready to move forward.

While Bobby was off considering his future, Howard flipped through the pictures. "How did you get these surveillance pictures from the feds?"

Mario pointed at the pictures. "The two children with the backpacks? I took them this morning at seven-thirty on Esplanade Avenue. They were waiting for the school bus. The FBI logo on the back of the pictures? That's a rubber stamp we use when forwarding documents to the local FBI office."

"Slick move," Howard smiled.

"We know they're running kids," Mario said. "Just don't know who they are."

In the limousine, Mario took a call from Glenn Macy. An appointment he set up between Glenn and the mayor had just finished. Garrett was overwhelmed that the Big Easy Voice gave him a column on the front page for a message to the people about why casinos are good for the people. Ten days of free positive messaging on the front page—the mayor couldn't buy that space. Mario made it happen.

"Mario—he loves the idea," Glenn said. "Another exclusive, thanks."

It was the first step in making the deal work, and Glenn had played a big part in making it come together.

At the top of the stairs, Julie appeared and gave a thumbs-up, dressed in an outfit that would get the mayor's attention. She knocked back a cocktail in the limo, not to curb her nerves, she was a professional—worries never came into play. She was celebrating Mario's success for conning a crime lord. She agreed—it'd pay off for everyone.

Mario alerted Garrett that the representative of the East Coast Meat Packing Company and Food Distributors was on her way.

Fifteen minutes later, the limousine pulled curbside at city hall. Julie climbed the steps of the building with the confidence that everyone was viewing her from the rear—she was right.

"Mr. Mayor, it's a pleasure to meet you," Julie said. Usually she didn't talk to her marks. She'd shoot them in the head and walk away. It was a first for her to take good news to someone for a change.

They chatted. Eye contact was made several times. Julie encouraged Garrett's flirtatious smile, as it played into her presentation.

"Mr. Mayor, my company is prepared to offer you some assistance in bringing casino gaming to your city in a grand way that will make you proud."

"Mario said your company is the backbone of the food and beverage supplies for casinos in Atlantic City."

"Correct, for many years." Then Julie laid out her plan.

The East Coast company would modernize a building in the Warehouse District, solely as a supplier for New

Orleans casinos. The company would purchase all the meats, products, beverages, beer, and liquor from local vendors. It would warehouse and package products for daily deliveries to the casinos. The Boardwalk was much like the French Quarter with limited parking and narrow streets. This process would help keep the local businesses of the French Quarter and Canal Street clear for shoppers.

One delivery a day to the casinos with all the food and supplies needed to operate—not ten or fifteen trucks throughout the day. It would eliminate traffic concerns, additional damage to streets, and not turn the city into a truck eyesore. If the mayor named her company as the food, beverage, and supply distributor, it would see that each local company continued operating with increased sales. The distribution warehouse would employ 150 people. An added bonus would be 100,000 dollars spent on advertising to get the mayor's voice to the people. TV, radio, and newspapers would be flooded with positive reasoning over the next week.

The smile left Garrett's face as he moved from flirting to business mode. "What's in it for your company?"

"We can buy in volume from each vendor, more than one casino could, and still resell the product at a value. If not done this way, each casino would pay for additional warehouse space, delivery trucks, and equipment. And jam your streets during deliveries."

Garrett had no comeback. The East Coast company had a good rating with the Boardwalk casinos. Owned by some businessmen in New York with an excellent reputation of value products and following through on every promise.

Not public was where the money came from to start the company, how it drove other suppliers out of the city, and who called the shots for the company.

The corporation was solid, paid taxes, employed many people, and was the most successful legit business the Ferrari family had operating. Now, all under the control of Bobby Galeffi. The mayor of New Orleans was about to make a deal with the devil himself.

Garrett walked Julie to the door. They shook hands, made a little eye contact, and he said he'd be in touch. She wasn't even back in the limousine when Mario got a call from him. Wanted his guarantee the company could deliver. Mario told him not to trust only him—make a call to the mayor of Atlantic City. Garrett had called and that was the problem—he could find nothing negative.

Companies that successful have bones in their closets. Mario wanted to tell him to look harder. If it produced a drug-free city—it was a good trade-off.

A week later, the mayor held a press conference. Mario and Howard sat in the front row. He announced the name of the company that was awarded the license for distribution to casinos in New Orleans. Garrett took credit for putting in place a distributor for food and beverages to ease traffic, increase employment, and generate millions of dollars in tax revenue for the city.

Introduced was the president of the East Coast company, which was the holding company for all the casino distributions. He made promises the mayor hoped he'd honor.

Garrett gave Mario and Howard a nod and that was all the recognition they wanted.

"Are we bad people?" Mario asked Howard.

"Was Robin Hood bad? We made a deal with the devil to take his drug business elsewhere."

"It's only a matter of time for Bobby G. to squeeze the vendors out and takeover himself," Mario said.

"It's a trade-off," Howard replied. "Squeezing out vendors or keeping drugs off the streets. The mayor had to choose what's best for the city."

CHAPTER 37

A FLEET OF LIMOUSINES left the building and Mario and Howard got in the last car. One headed to the car wash and picked up Big Gabe and Cyrus. Another picked up Jay at the Royal Street Grocery store, then stopped at Riverside Inn and Zack, Dave, Emma Lou, and Pearl Ann took to the back seat. In Howard's car, he and Mario sat in the back and celebrated the occasion with champagne. At the curb of One Shell Square stood Ralph Givens. He climbed in and handed Mario an envelope.

"The taxes are paid on your money," Ralph said. "The investment account is deleted and the balance deposited to the account of "Not Forgotten" with enough money to operate for two years..

Howard's limo made one more stop and picked up Roxy and Glenn.

At ten A.M. sharp, the limousines rolled up to what was an old nuns convent. When the building was purchased with the detective's investment funds, the place was falling apart and was an eyesore for the neighborhood. Now, it was put back together like new with shiny painted shutters, new walkways, and the inside turned into housing for fifty people. There were also a bank of restrooms and showers and a kitchen to feed many throughout the day.

Howard and Mario walked the red carpet into the house, where their friends and business partners who made this happen awaited their arrival. With champagne glasses raised, Mario made a toast to Jay and Cyrus. "Your new home."

Earlier, a busload of homeless were dropped off and introduced to the showers, donated toiletries, and fresh clothes. They joined in the party.

The word had spread of Mario and Howard's involvement in making this happen. While they denied it, they gave a wink of an eye to their closest friends.

Mario took the floor one more time, expressing his gratitude to the residents of Riverside Inn, namely Zack, Dave, Emma Lou, and Pearl Ann, for their support in putting the endeavor together.

"It was a joint effort," Mario shouted. The Riverside Inn crew took a bow.

Champagne was passed and Roxy and girls from her nightclub performed. A line of dancers took to the floor when Roxy opened with her rendition of Sister Sledge, "We Are Family."

"Not forgotten!" The two detectives shouted with glasses in the air. It was a jumpstart in solving the homeless problem in New Orleans. Those who knew the story of how the house came about had tears in their eyes. Mario and Howard kept sipping their champagne to drown their emotions. After all, tough detectives don't cry.

The End

AUTHORS NOTES

Many readers have written me, and I'm always happy to hear from them. I've been asked, Is that true? Did that happen? Where is the restaurant you wrote about in New Orleans? My books are based around New Orleans, and there are more to come.

I'm always happy to share with my readers more about the locations mentioned in the chapters and what encouraged me to write about a street, a building, a restaurant, or a person. Here are a few places that appear in this book.

Chapter One: New Orleans Police Department, Eighth District. Located at 334 Royal Street, New Orleans.

Chapter Nine: Breads on Oak. A cozy, artisan bakery with organic breads baked in a stone-hearth oven, also serves pastries, muffins, soups, and sandwiches. Located at 8640 Oak Street, New Orleans.

Chapter Ten: Schoen funeral home. On March 4, 1874, Jacob Schoen and Henry Frantz started a family business at 155 N. Peters Street and adopted as their policy "the highest standard of funeral service to all, regardless of financial circumstance." In 1897, Frantz sold his interest to Schoen. Jacob's son, Philip, became a partner and the firm was renamed Jacob Schoen & Son. The current business is located at 3827 Canal Street, New Orleans.

Chapter Fourteen: Dixie Brewing Company. A regional brewery founded in New Orleans in 1907. Its beer is brewed at what used to be the only remaining large volume brewery within the city of New Orleans. During Prohibition, its name was the "Dixie Beverage Company." Currently, it's owned by Gayle Benson, owner of the New Orleans Saints football team and the New Orleans Pelicans basketball team, along with Joe and Kendra Bruno. Located at 2401 Tulane Avenue, New Orleans.

Chapter Fourteen: Lafayette Square. Designed in 1788 and named for French aristocrat Gilbert du Motier, Marquis de Lafayette, it is the second-oldest public park (Jackson Square is the oldest) in New Orleans. Located between St. Charles Avenue and Camp Street in the Central Business District.

Chapter Fifteen: Le Pavillon Hotel. A historic hotel, built in 1907. Located at 833 Poydras Street, New Orleans.

Chapter Nineteen: Venezia Restaurant. A family-friendly place for classic, old-school Italian fare, including pizza cooked in a stone oven. Located at 134 N. Carrollton Avenue, New Orleans.

Chapter Twenty-Three: Liuzza's by the Track. A mid-city grill and casual Creole tavern for gumbo, corned beef, locally made sausage, and signature BBQ shrimp po'boys. Located at 1518 N. Lopez Street, New Orleans.

Chapter Twenty-Seven: Antoine's Restaurant. Built in 1840, renowned French-Creole cuisine, birthplace of Oysters Rockefeller. Located at 713 Saint Louis Street, New Orleans.

Chapter Thirty-Five: Ruth's Chris Steak House. In 1965, Ruth Fertel, a single mom looking for an opportunity, saw a New Orleans steak house for sale in the classifieds. She took a chance and mortgaged her home and purchased Chris Steak House. Later the name was changed to Ruth's Chris Steak House and spread to over 150 restaurants worldwide. The restaurant in New Orleans is located in Harrah's at 525 Fulton Street.

I love to write, and I love to hear from my readers. If you enjoyed this book or any of my others, send me an email, and I will respond.

Please help me as an independent author and leave a review on Amazon. I appreciate your time in doing so.

vito@vitozuppardobooks.com
www.vitozuppardobooks.com

Thank you!

ABOUT THE AUTHOR

Vito Zuppardo retired in 2003, after twenty-five years in the casino business, where he recruited high-limit gaming customers for various casinos around the world.

Vito started writing in 1986, collecting pieces of information from each trip to Las Vegas, the Bahamas, Monte Carlo, and the many other places where he represented casinos. His primary job was keeping his clients happy, while they were vacationing at luxury casino resorts. His first two books, *Tales of Lady Luck* and *Alluring Lady Luck*, are based on true events from his experiences during his casino days. He is the author of eight books including the Voodoo Lucy Series and the True Blue Detective Series.

VOODOO LUCY SERIES
BOOK 2
REVENGE

CHAPTER 1

Even with Lucy's eyes wide open, it was dark. A blindfold tightly tied around her head prevented even a shadow of light from peeking through. The feel of the covering is coarse as it pressed against her face. Musty smell from the cloth wasn't overwhelming but differently something she wouldn't forget. Listening for any sound that might give a location, a car, train, or people talking in the distance. The deafening sound of silence was almost scary. There were no clues other than her shoes dragging the dirt ground—maybe an old garage or barn. The strong hand that held her by the arm was large, rough and thick skin. Her other hand clutched to Karen Foster a lifelong friend walked step for step with Lucy, until her hand was jerked away. It was the last contact she'd have with her friend.

The last thing she remembered was walking down a dirt road with Karen talking about fourteen-year-old stuff. She recalled a black pickup truck pulled to the side of the road. Not making eye contact her and Karen continued.

A hand wrapped around both their nose, and their knees buckled—falling in and out of consciousness.

Using all her senses was self-taught, but this was the first time being blindfold. Most times men told her to turn around or close your eyes when taking advantage of her.

She knew time had passed but didn't remember events between unconsciousness. The sweet smell that took her breath away dissipated.

The heat was intense a barn fire maybe, but it couldn't be—she was they were in a building. The sound of steel banging together and heat intensifying, there was no doubt in her mind she stood in front of an incinerator.

A solid clang sounded when the steel door closed. Then the heat intensified the door must have been open now, ran through young Lucy's mind. Knowing better than to scream, it would only get her a smack and a rag in the mouth making sure it didn't happen again.

A voice she recognized but couldn't place for sure kept saying something like a crawdad making her thing the heat was coming from a pot boiling crawfish. If so the smell of garlic, crab boil, and seasoning would have been evident—there was no such smell. With a deep snort a horrible smell came over her—nothing she'd ever sensed before.

Tears flowed down her face, her dress wet from perspiration, clutched her body. She let out a scream, then another.

"Lucy, on the count of three, you will wake up," Doctor Griffin said. "One, two, three."

Lucy sat up her heart racing and a horrified look on her face. With one hand, she brushed her damp hair away from her eyes. Then a calm came over her as she twisted her long red hair into a curl, a dead giveaway. It didn't fool Dr. Griffin.

"Lucinda, let me talk to Lucy," he said.

"This is Lucy," Lucinda said.

"At the sound of the bell. Lucy will be at full attention," he said. "Do you understand Lucinda?"

"She's weak, I can help her," Lucinda said.

The doctor hit a small desk bell. It rang with a ding. Immediately Lucy responded with tears flowing rapidly from her eyes over her rosy cheeks across her lips. The doctor handed her tissue and a glass of water the usual preparation for when Lucy awakes from hypnosis.

"How did I do?" Lucy asked between snuffles.

"About the same," he said relaxing back in his chair. Even a psychiatrist, as well-trained as Dr. Griffin can be fatigued after a thirty-minute session dealing with multiple personalities. "Your mind shut down, in the same part of the story."

Lucy freshened her makeup and ran a comb through her hair. "Maybe it's for the best."

"We have to address Lucinda," Dr. Griffin said writing a note into his journal. "Until Lucinda is out of your mind or at least controllable, anything is possible. None of which is healthy," he lifted his head to see Lucy gazing up at the sun beaming through the transom window above his head. "Lucy? We're on the same page?"

"Yes, Dr. Griffin," She said shrugging her shoulders like a child. "I'll get Lucinda under control." Something she'd said after every session. She'd never used the mind manipulating tools taught by the doctor or took the medication he insisted needed to control her multiple personality disorder.

Fairly sure her problems started with Karen's older brother Johnny, at least she thinks so. She was young—lured into a garage with him, to look for some toy or game she wasn't sure. Can you remember things passed the age of six? Maybe that's what Dr. Griffin meant by mind blocking. Allowing you to suppress emotions you're not ready to face visibly or remember the traumatic event. One day Lucinda will allow Lucy to tell the doctor the entire series of encounters with the bad people she grew up with in Tupelo Mississippi, for now, Lucinda will shield Lucy of the pain.

Dr. Griffin turned the doorknob gently to let Lucy into the empty waiting room. Even his receptionist had left for the evening as she had often done when sessions ran long, and no other appointments were scheduled.

"Lucy? Please take your medication," he said pulling her arm gently for attention.

With the other hand, she curled her hair repeatedly then smiled back at the doctor, "I'll take care of her," Lucinda said, "and you ever touch her again. I'll slit your throat."

The doctor quickly dropped her arm. An innocent touch or gesture is the very thing that will set a patient off, spinning them out of control in a downward spiral. "I'm sorry Lucy, I was just making a point."

Lucy left a check at the front counter and picked up a reminder appointment card the receptionist had left for the next week. As usual, she'd be a no-show—until her nightmares become uncontrollable, then she'd beg Dr. Griffin for another session.

Lucy strolled down Royal Street exchanging pleasant smiles and handshakes. Stopping to give a phony laugh at a store owner's joke, the same one he'd told her three times. It was her way to get on with the day and show Lucinda her visit with Dr. Griffin gave Lucy her power back. For now, Lucinda would crawl back into the dark hole she lived in only to surface when Lucy least expected or needed help.

CHAPTER 2

Mostly, Lucy's life was rolling along. All aspects of the business were good, the legal ones and her business that walked the fine line of the law and often crossed.

Stella James, a vice cop with the New Orleans Police Department, bloomed into a little more than good friends, thanks to Mario DeLuca. An introduction a year earlier allowed Lucy to run a scam with assistance from the police, without them ever knowing. It took a bad guy off the street and confirmed to another client that Lucy had Voodoo powers.

Stella and Lucy had been out a few times, neither wanted to call it a date. Cocktails at a Jazz Bar and dinner ended with a walk-through Jackson Square. A kiss goodnight and they would go their separate ways.

Stella always made time from her cop duties to meet Lucy after a session with Dr. Griffin. She didn't know all the details of what brought Lucy to treatment, but after sitting with a police therapist for justifiably killing a man while on the job, she couldn't only imagine what it would be like under hypnotist having a psychiatrist rife you with questions. This day they were to meet on a bench across from Saint Louis Cathedral. Stella introduced Lucy to cannoli's from Brocato's bakery and it quickly became a favorite. Today's visit was coffee and a cannoli for each. It should get a smile from Lucy—she thought.

Lucy arrived in a huff, took a seat not saying a word. Her usual actions for the first hour after visiting Dr. Griffin. Stella, her rock, shoulder to lean on, all around good friend took the brunt of the shit storm that came after a session.

"I've got your favorite," Stella said handing a cannoli and coffee.

Lucy frowned motioned for her to place it on the bench, "thanks—you know this stuff goes right to my hip."

"That's me, Lucy," Stella said. "Beefing you up, all one hundred and ten pounds of you."

Stella waited, and it came as it had every week. Big tears streamed down Lucy's face speaking but not making much sense. Their heads rested on each other's shoulders. That was Stella's clue to break out a small box of tissue she carried to Dr. Griffin's after party.

"I take it didn't go well," Stella whispered.

"No," Lucy said lifting her head. "I can't remember behind the heat I felt on my face. Same as the time before and the time before that."

Stella always weighted her words with this topic, "maybe it's your brain's way of telling you, you're not ready."

"Ready for what?" Lucy wiped her eyes with a tissue. "Can it be any worse if the doctor pushed forward?"

"Honey, the little I know—it could be a lot worse. That's why they're doctors," Stella said giving her a kiss on the cheek. "He'll know when you're ready. Let's finish up, and I'll walk you back to the salon."

A half of box of tissue later Lucy's tears were under control, and she knocked back the rest of the coffee and the remainder of the cannoli. Both touched up their lipstick sharing a little gold compact mirror. With a big puff, Lucy exhaled taking Stella's hand. It was Lucy's way of saying she was ready to put the doctor's session behind her.

They strolled the uneven concrete up Pirate Alley to Royal Street hand and hand. "You're just what the doctor ordered," Lucy said. "Coffee, cannoli, and a shoulder to cry on."

Stella pulled her closer and gave a kiss on her cheek, "I'm here for you any time and place. You need to let me in, I can help."

Lucy smiled and gave a squeeze of her hand, but that was as far as it would go. Her life was too complicated. Therapy sessions, Zack Nelson chasing her down for the bank job her father pulled, the after-hour business she inherited from Vivien, and the police have yet to discover she killed Picklehead.

They stopped in front of the salon. Lucy smiled and looked into Stella's eyes. She could be the one, but Lucy came with too much baggage. "Stella, you couldn't handle me."

"Give me a try," Stella said pulling her by the hand.

Then she went for it and laid into her with a kiss. It was a passionate one—the type you do in private. Their mouths slid across the fresh slippery lipstick. This time Lucy didn't pull away. The embrace lasted and with every second that passed Stella watched from the corner of her eye the woman of her dream's fingers twirling her red hair around into a long tight curl. Her hand gracefully rested on her shoulder and fiddled the hair in place. This was not the shy woman Stella knew, but she was game.

They broke apart. Stella's big brown eye flickered. "Wow."

"When you want loving, call on Lucinda," she said running her tongue over her lips. "I'm your girl." Then she stepped in the salon as a customer walked out.

Stella's head was spinning. It made no sense to her, "call who?"

Made in United States
North Haven, CT
22 May 2023